THE PATH OF LEAST RESISTANCE

LEAH DOWNING

The Path of Least Resistance

Leah Downing Books are available for order through Ingram Press Catalogues.

This book is a work of fiction. Names, characters, places, and incidents are either products of the author's imagination or are used fictitiously. Any resemblance to actual events or locales, or persons, living or dead, is entirely coincidental. Some aspects of this story fall under the definition of Historical Fiction; whereas, true characteristics of the time period and events have been borrowed, but story and character(s) are fictitious.

Printed in the United States of America

Published by Full Net Enterprises

For more information on future works, events, and blogs visit:
Facebook: Leah Downing Author
Twitter: @ledowningauthor

ISBN-13: 978-0-9977323-1-3

www.529Books.com
Editor: Lisa Cerasoli
Interior Design: Danielle Canfield
Cover Design: Claire Moore

Praise for
The Path of Least Resistance
Book Two of The Shooting Stars Series
#1 Amazon Bestseller

★★★★★
—A Very Entertaining Read—

"The storytelling in *The Path of Least Resistance* is unique in its ability to weave through genres like homeland security, romance, and the supernatural without batting an eye or losing any of the realism that's required to fully embrace the struggles these characters are going through. Downing has a special ability to immerse the reader in every scene and every character she writes. Her dialogue and writing style are so in sync that there's rarely a dull moment."

—Kenneth Atchity
Literary Manager, Producer, Author
The Story Merchant

★★★★★
—This is a Series I am Beyond Excited About—

"Leah Downing has successfully followed up her debut novel with another fascinating story combining real-life successes and failures with suspicion and the paranormal. Her dialogue is honest and exciting and possesses a natural flow. I already loved the character of Lauren, but after reading *The Path of Least Resistance*, I have an entirely new and stronger respect for her."

—Jen Thomason
Dandelions Inspired: Reading & Reviewing Amazing Books!

★★★★★
—AMAZING…ADDICTIVE…and not to be missed—

"Be prepared to immediately pick up *Catch a Falling Star* to read again once you finish *The Path of Least Resistance!*"

— Jesse Neidt
Intuitive Consultant
http://www.jesseneidt.com/

For Mom

★★★★★
—Catch a Falling Star is a Must Read—

"I loved *Catch a Falling Star*! I couldn't put it down. It's hard to believe that this is Leah Downing's first book! She is highly skilled at engaging the reader by developing intriguing characters and creating unexpected twists and turns in the storyline that keep you on the edge of your seat and wanting more!"

— S. McGuinness

★★★★★
—Best Book I've Read in a Long Time—

"This is what a page turner is all about. It has something in it for everyone, a great love story, suspense, thriller and comedy all wrapped into one phenomenal book. I cannot wait to get my hands on the next one!"

—KashP

★★★★★
—Heart Pounding Movement & Intrigue—

"Fast paced, intriguing heart pounding movement that splashes with tactile imagery. Leah commands the scenes with rich detail and authority. It is fun & funny without skipping a beat of juicy detail, weaving in mystery beyond worlds. Bravo!"

—Kesha Engel

★★★★★
—Best Romance Novel I've Read in Years—

"*Catch a Falling Star* is so much more than just a love story. It layers mystery with hope, passion with fear, and adventure with legends of supernatural forces. It draws you into the world of Lauren St Germain and James Bayer. I can't wait to read Book Two: *The Path of Least Resistance*."

—Dr. Cindy Mann

THE PATH OF LEAST RESISTANCE

"He created man from clay like pottery. And He created the djinn from a smokeless flame of fire."

Koran AR-Rahman 55:14–15

"And we sought to reach Heaven, but found it's filled with strong angels and shooting stars."

Koran Sher Ali 72:8

prologue

"The red djinn have one purpose: the downfall of the human race. They are the followers of Iblis, and from the shadows, slowly influence humanity's thoughts over the centuries. Red djinn are the true terrorists of the universe—they whisper in the ears of men and women, causing them to take actions that are against the laws of God and man."[1]

The Lucifer story in the Bible and the Iblis story in the Koran follow the same bent. In the Bible, Lucifer and his followers are thrown out of Heaven by God; "The Fall." In the Koran, Iblis was thrown out of Heaven by Allah. Both Lucifer and Iblis were exiled for displaying too much pride. Once banished to Earth, Lucifer had permission to tempt humans. Same with Iblis, he was granted the power to lead humans astray from the Creator's love. Lucifer is a fallen angel. Iblis, however, is not an angel. The Koran designates djinn as a separate race from angels.

---

[1] Rosemary Ellen Guiley & Philip J. Imbrogno, *The Vengeful Djinn: Unveiling the Hidden Agendas of Genies*, (Woodbury: Llewellyn Publications, 2011), 82.

Neither a singular djinni nor the djinn collective can physically force an action. Still, they are extremely powerful and very cunning. Most westerners associate them with genies, like the ones portrayed in the Disney Picture *Aladdin.* There are four types of djinn: red, blue, black, and yellow. Each group possesses different personality traits and levels of power, but all djinn share certain characteristics. Djinn are tricksters who tend to be vindictive and self-serving. None can perform true miracles; their talent lies in the illusion of miracles. They create visions—wishes, future events, fantasies, military strategies—so real that the human experiencing it can't discern the vision from reality. The most revered rank of djinn is the red order with which entanglement should be avoided. At all costs. The red leader, a djinni by the name of Iblis, is the most powerful djinn in existence.

PART I

c h a p t e r   o n e

Fredon Township, New Jersey
AUGUST 18, 1983

The last time Collin was told to change one of the bulbs on the porch, about three weeks ago, it wasn't burnt out; it had merely been unscrewed halfway. Collin suspected that was the case again as he walked to the porch. He unscrewed that same bulb, the one in the middle of the track, and shook it close to his ear while holding the fresh bulb in his other hand. He heard nothing. Screwed it back in tight, flipped the switch, and the entire front porch was illuminated. He went back inside to his dad.

His father's eyes narrowed. Without commenting, he took the new bulb from his son's hand and returned it to a shelf in the closet.

Coming back from a friend's later that night, Collin noticed that same middle light had gone dark again. With his attention drawn up to the porch light, he stepped in dog shit as he veered off the path to the door. He then turned and went around to the right side of the house. Collin uncoiled the hose and put a hand on the shutter of the window to keep his balance as he scraped the bottom of his shoe on the siding. He managed to kick the soiled shoe off and reach for the hose while standing on one foot.

A faint groan came from just inside.

Scared it was a ghost, possibly the Red One that sometimes visits, he froze. A cricket chirped, which startled him into clasping onto the shutter with both hands as he sucked in his breath. Dampness immediately spread through the bottom of his sock when he set his foot down in the mulch without thinking.

Another groan. A moan. A woman.

"Nadine," an unfamiliar male's voice slid her name across the breeze, "you're incorrigible."

Then a rhythmic rocking grew in volume. Even though Collin did not fully comprehend the meaning behind it, it made him uncomfortable. Instinctively, he crouched down and prayed his father wasn't coming home anytime soon.

The happenings going on from inside the house were associated with the word "romp," per his aunt. Collin's eyes filled with hot tears, but he didn't want to cry. If his dad caught wind of those tears on the brims of his lashes, then lashes it would be for the boy. One tear would equal one blow.

Try not to leave streaks on the cheeks.

"These women…." At his dad's voice, Collin turned around. His dad was transfixed on the window.

Collin's gaze shot back down. "Sir," he peeped.

"We're cursed with them. My mom, your mom, you'll probably marry one, too. Beautiful…cursed women."

Collin's face reddened.

"Go on," Dad instructed, almost as an afterthought. "Never mind your shoe and get Aunt Mikki. Go to her. Stay there for a day or two."

Collin bit the insides of his cheeks so hard he tasted blood. Fortunately, Dad's eyes were focused on the window, not the hot tear dripping off his chin.

Aunt Micki was less than a mile away. He flew over the back roads in a straight line there. After a few days, she informed him that his mom was no longer contagious and he could go back home.

Mom was stiff the first month back, both physically and emotionally. She came around eventually as gardening took over her free time. Beautiful flowers framed the house, starting at the area in front of the den. She painted it over with colorful splendor to mask the shit under the surface.

c h a p t e r   t w o

Saudi Arabian Desert
FEBRUARY 23, 1991

The modern-day warriors congregated under a huge camo net, hot and dirty, with the undiluted smell of BO emitting from the forty-five or so Marines gathered for the final meeting regarding *Task Force Ripper*. LtCol Mattis and his aid were going over the final details of their mission to be initiated the following morning from their current position.

Not so known to fall for anyone's bullshit these days, Cpl Collin St. Germain was the youngest in the group. His broad shoulders created the perfect frame for his worn uniform and his wide-legged stance challenged anyone to speak to him without respect. As impressive as he appeared, his insides were authentically a bundle of raw nerves.

Collin's dark hair, now faded to a sandy tan, normally required a regulation "high and tight" but that infraction was of minimal importance in the middle of nowhere. They were all in the same boat because of months in the Saudi Arabian sandbox of isolation. The briefing was eclipsed by a singular line of thought running through Collin's mind. The importance of this transmission ripped through Collin's head and reverberated throughout his being.

The hairs on his neck bristled as he became aware that his physical body was being used as a conduit of sorts to some other parallel universe. It seemed as if he were the only one there who heard the loud ringing.

It was inescapable, but no one else seemed to notice it.

There was something so uncomfortably simplistic about the LtCol's plan that it was causing this overwhelming, otherworldly, reaction in Collin. He knew with all certainty that should they follow these orders, he would not make it through the next day with his life.

None of them would.

The usually rowdy group was silent as the LtCol droned on. He broke down the poorly planned route of moving due north into Kuwait.

Collin's throat began to burn. The words were going to vomit out and he would be completely disgraced;

however, even the fear of certain humiliation couldn't silence what happened next.

"Sir, I apologize, sir, but I need to suggest an alternative route."

Fuck me.

LtCol Mattis strutted directly over to Collin and dropped the open map of the Arabian Peninsula with a deliberate smack on the picnic table. "What's that, Corporal?" LtCol Mattis was ready to shred this NCO to ribbons.

Collin smelled the burnt coffee on the LtCol's breath.

Guided by some transcendental influence, Collin broke all protocol, and pointed to a different route on the map. "Here," he spoke right to the commanding officer's eye. "It's shorter and further away from the most populated Iraqi base camp up north. The Iraqis are not anticipating that we have any other objective except to march north, head on to Kuwait City." Collin didn't falter in his conviction. "Sir, we must reroute by first moving north on forty-seven degrees thirty minutes east longitude 'til it intersects the twenty-ninth north parallel right on the border. From that point, we can roll northeast on the shortest route into Kuwait City. The Iraqis are not expecting this. They know of our current path— to head straight north from our position here. And they are ready for us. They've built up their troops in Ash

Subayhiyah, and those last capable Iraqi units are ready to engage us from all directions. We'll be caught in the choke points of their minefields. Sir, it's no secret that we're moving forward with a confrontation. There needs to be a change; we must execute the path of least resistance." Collin tapped his finger on the N 29.00, E 47.30 by co-ordinates on the map.

Without looking at Collin's finger or the map, LtCol Mattis responded, "They will expect us to have the ability to move faster now, so it's reasonable to assume that they're anticipating our switch to your route." LtCol Mattis spoke in a tone which insinuated he and St. Germain were in the middle of a private conversation. The familiarity of it caused something inside Collin to click—the LtCol had already considered this alternate and much more secure route.

Collin wasn't going to let the LtCol knowingly lean on an unfounded rumor when it came to this critical mission. "There's no Intel which supports the Iraqis have any knowledge of the new 'three-shot' line charge."

LtCol Mattis trembled so slightly that only Collin perceived his apprehension.

As if the unconventional interruption never took place, LtCol Mattis returned to the podium at the head of the meeting and changed the course. There was no appreciation, no glory, for Collin or his astute observation. Perhaps because Collin did not propose an enlightened idea; in fact, Collin's plan was a straightforward, sound maneuver, causing Collin and the rest of his platoon unrest since LtCol Mattis must have disregarded it before the briefing had even begun. Even the wind rippling the camo net slowed, as if allowing silence, to assist the mythical eavesdroppers lurking in outlying desert.

Once everyone was up to speed on the new primary route of assault, LtCol Mattis ended the briefing with an order that Collin would never forget. "When we get to that first minefield and begin our breach, if any of yous start seeing little brown heads popping up, you turn 'em into jelly!"

All eyes remained forward and LtCol Mattis abruptly announced it was time for the logistics team to gather in his tent for a more focused meeting.

No one flinched as everyone stood at attention waiting for LtCol Mattis to exit the space. As he resentfully brushed past Collin, the LtCol delivered this quick message: "You'll keep your spot as the lead breaching element. Your team will still clear those goddamned minefields."

Walking back to his vehicle, Collin sucked in the first real breath he'd taken in hours. A handful of other Marines and LCpl Marshall Mayhem fell into step with him. No one uttered a word until they were out of earshot of the others.

Mayhem broke the silence with a declaration of awe. "Holy shit, Grover."

Collin shakily pulled a cigarette from his left breast pocket. "Fuck," was all he could manage as he cupped the Zippo to get a much-needed drag.

chapter three

The next morning, the brutal force of Collin's sexual frustration was pent up in aggravation that mercilessly grated on him, especially when it was windy. And on this day, the day they would roll into Kuwait City, the wind showed no mercy.

In the lead position, Collin's task was to spearhead the first line of AAVs on this new path, the one he had essentially changed the night before. More specifically, he would command the first AAV to the edge of the first minefield. From this point, he would call out on the radio that the line charge was armed and ready to deploy.

Under the cover of darkness in the wee hours of the morning prior to the mission, Collin's mind practiced the firing of that first line charge over and over in his head. As he rehearsed the scenario, he chain-smoked cigarettes that he'd torn the filters from, and let burn down to his calloused fingertips.

He was ready.

He was ready to go.

After all, this new path was his brainchild...he'd better be ready.

If there was a misfire or even the slightest mistake, he'd rather die in the attempt of making it to Kuwait, rather than live through a defeat. There was an endless line of AAVs staged behind him filled with the lives of countless young Marines. They depended upon him to find the minefield's edge and create a path for safe passage. Making it to Kuwait City alive was key.

As the sun teased a shimmer in the sky, the Marines efficiently geared up into their positions to roll into the desert expanse. Miles of the terrifying and featureless unknown. The moment one's guard is down a mine is hit and life-ending carnage has occurred before anyone would even know what happened.

Collin still didn't know just how the fuck he had ended up here.

He thought of those genies living in magic lamps out in desert caves, granting wishes to those who found them. If he could have one wish, what would it be? One of those few precious days of freedom with Stephanie before he left for this hell....

She rolled a small ball of sticky hashish into a bowl and passed it over her exposed breasts for him. "Do you really have to go?" she asked as her hand cupped his already hard dick. She gave it a gentle tug—a gesture that screamed of ripping the cord holding his climax.

He took a long drag, feeling the syrupy burn scratch his throat before he relaxed into ambivalence. "Yes."

Her pouted expression communicated the volume of sexual acts she wished him to perform instead of leaving for the nasty brown desert the following day. He didn't respond, but rolled over and slid his hand down her petal soft belly to part her already damp crevice.

"Grover!" Mayhem hollered with agitation from the rear crew compartment. He had a death grip on the radio where overlapping voices furiously questioned why their AAV, first in line, had not yet come to a fucking halt.

Their lone AAV had inched past the co-ordinates and into the first known minefield.

"Give the command to stop, bro!" he yelled at Collin.

"That wish could be granted now," slithered into Collin's head with such clarity that he glanced around to see if anyone else heard it.

"Halt!" Collin commanded.

A collective sigh of both relief and aggravation wasn't masked among the three other men assigned to Collin's AAV, nor was the string of obscenities that blasted through the radio. The collective of heavy armor had stopped short of the deadly area to wait as Collin's AAV breached the inner boundary where he would release the first line charge to clear the field. The looming explosive path was the territory that Collin had the honor to secure for his country. The others held back in an orderly fashion until it was safe to trudge forward.

Collin manned the armored sacrificial lamb. If a mine was buried before the expected target, he would detonate it, and take the hit for the greater good. Should that happen—the destruction of Collin and his men— the next AAV would move past the wreckage to complete the mission.

And should that second one be destroyed, the next one would move forward.

And so on.

With Collin's head back in the game and his testosterone levels amped from Mayhem blaring Black Sabbath's "Paranoid" in their hull, he turned to the crew and yelled, "Are you fucking ready?"

Mayhem, seated at the base of the sidewinder missile that would launch the devastation ahead, grabbed his crotch. "Yeah, fuck yeah!"

"Go time!"

The four men initiated the sequence they'd practiced in training a hundred times before. The pressure was on with such large numbers of tanks and AAVs lined up behind them—all sitting ducks ready to be targeted by Iraqi artillery and fired upon at any moment. The tension was skyrocketing, as the tick tock of the timer grew more ominous by the second.

Mayhem popped up the cover protecting the switch that armed the sidewinder missile attached to the top of the AAV. It looked just like a kitchen light switch…with balls. With a shit-eating grin, he flipped the switch up and pressed the button labeled FIRE The force from the sidewinder being propelled off the AAV jerked the whole vehicle with a thrust equal to a 7.0 on the Richter Scale.

Collin's lungs magnetized to his back, ripping all the oxygen out of them, which, in turn created a heavy lead sensation bottoming out into his groin. He forced his irritated, watery eyes to remain open so he could focus on the shaky but straight line of rope shooting 120 meters out in front of them. The 1750-pound line charge landed in a massive thud across the minefield detonating along with it every mine within eight meters on both sides of its path. The incredible explosion rocked even the furthest vehicle back from Collin's.

Collin's AAV, the Guinea pig at the front of the line, lurched forward, seething in confidence from its aluminum hull. Once Collin's group made it through the winding track cleared ahead, the other iron giants rolled up behind. With caution the parade commenced, following in the precise tracks Collin had created; there was no room for deviation.

Everything was precisely timed so that Collin could reach the end of the 120 meters and clear the next length just as the others came up behind him to keep the task force moving along. No more sitting ducks.

Completely in his element, Mayhem flipped the switch and boldly pressed the FIRE button once more. They braced for the violent jerk and watched as the rope launched and landed.

Nothing.

The traffic jam behind them flooded the radio traffic, all demanding, "How come there weren't any more goddammed explosions?!"

The last thing Collin recalled hearing was, "You can't put this fucking line in reverse!"

In the same amount of time it took Collin to turn to Mayhem and shout the order, Mayhem was already up and snapping his chinstrap. Mayhem grabbed his engineer kit and pushed out the back hatch.

Collin knocked his head on an extraneous piece of metal as he clumsily dropped back down in the TC's hatch to watch through the glass vision blocks. Mayhem bolted across the desert to the first block of C4 on the defective line charge. In vain, Collin rubbed the sleeve of his Chemical Protective Suit in a circular motion over the three-inch-thick glass block. They'd been tinged by smoke from the burning oil fields to the north.

Like a man running for his life (because he was) Mayhem almost skidded past the first block of C4 at the twenty-meter mark. He caught himself by driving his knee into the sand, slowing his frantic sprint to an abrupt stop.

Muscle memory flew into overdrive as Mayhem clawed the crimping pliers from his pack. He used the punch end of them to poke a clean hole into the block. With hawk-like focus, he grabbed a non-electric blasting cap and shoved it into the hole he'd just made.

"Checkmate, motherfuckers!" was Mayhem's war cry as he pulled the ignitor before hauling ass back.

It was twenty meters back and he had sixty seconds. Walk in the park.

C'mon, Mayhem!

Mayhem had the swagger of a rock star about it all as he slammed the hatch behind him and shot up next to Collin to peer through the vision blocks. The men braced themselves.

The blasting cap did exactly what it was supposed to do—the chain reaction fired with brilliance, causing the entire length of the rope to blow.

They proceeded through that path, and then a third, without resistance.

The southern route to Kuwait City was clear for now.

The aerial assault of the Basra-Kuwait Highway began almost simultaneously, bombing the hell out of any remaining Iraqis attempting to leave north out of the city. It claimed the lives of thousands and resulted in miles of destroyed cars left abandoned along Highway 80 heading out of Kuwait City to Iraq, a.k.a. "The Highway of Death." The burnt-to-a-crisp, larger-than-life litter globally portrayed the absolute authority of the US military. Thus, victory was declared by Bush in an astounding one-hundred-hour war.

March 1, 1991

Dear Collin,

I know you are out there in that hellish sand pit representing for God and country. Your service is honorable and I'd be proud to call you my son. It is with a heavy heart and weighty conscience that I write this. While you've been gone, Steph has been frequenting Dan White's place, and not just to babysit his little girl, even though that's what she tells everyone. I thought it might pass over and it could be one of those "don't ask, don't tell" kind of things, but....
She's still planning the wedding. I'm so sorry.

I hope you enjoy the smokes and the candy. They said not to send chocolate, so I thought you'd like the gummy bears and beef jerky.

Godspeed, Lorena

c h a p t e r   f o u r

Vista, California
APRIL 16, 1991

Collin thought the revelation of Steph's infidelity with
Dan would be the peak of her vindictive burn. Unfortunately, it was only the first spark of several fires that he
needed to extinguish upon returning stateside.

Collin Andrew St. Germain
Unit 2315
320 Pomelo Drive
Vista, CA 92081

Dear Mr. St. Germain,
*You are hereby being pressured with a notice of evic-
tion to vacate the premises below on or before February 28,
1991.*

Sunset Springs Apartments, Inc. in the city of Vista, California

    The reason for this eviction notice is:
    (X) Your failure to pay rent due is in arrears. A demand for payment was made on Feb. 1, 1991, and you have refused to forward the necessary funds due for the rent during this period.

    You are hereby notified that if you make all outstanding payments before the date of eviction, you will be able to remain in the premises provided you continue to pay your rent in a timely manner.

    Signature
J. Marchette
Sunset Springs Properties, Inc.

It wasn't the notice on the door, but the stench coming from behind it that truly gave him pause. Collin held his breath as he turned the knob. The door opened halfway and then jammed. The trash bags blocking the entrance to the apartment stank of rotting food.

Collin turned to the side and squeezed through the opening, immediately feeling the heat. The air inside was not only foul, but hot and stale. No air conditioning. He kicked the bags aside and opened the door wider.

Flies circled the dishes piled up in the sink and scattered throughout the kitchen. Out of habit, he flipped the light switch. Nothing happened. He left the switch up and walked to the living room. Overflowing ashtrays, with a mix of tan and white filters, were perched everywhere. Cigarette burns dotted the perimeters of the ashtrays. A wall of empty beer cans had been built and Collin smacked it as he went to the bedroom. The cacophony of aluminum cans echoed in the empty space.

Most of his clothes were still folded in the drawers. The TV was gone. He shook out a trash bag and shoved his meager belongings in it. Caught between putting a hole in the particle board closet and screaming, the seams of the bag ripped and his clothes spilled out the bottom. When he kicked the pile, his foot easily shot through it—right into the base of the dresser. The pain set him off. He found his tool kit, still in the closet, pulled out a hammer, and pounded the closet door until it broke into splinters. He was losing the entire deposit anyway.

After exhausting his rage, he scooped up his clothes and left the apartment without looking back. He moved into the barracks and tried to keep his distance, but constant reminders of her were forwarded to him.

Collection agencies sent notices daily to his PO box on base. She hadn't paid the utilities for months. She took their cat to the vet constantly. She'd financed furniture on his credit and didn't tell him. She'd upgraded the diamond in her ring. She made the deposit on the venue for their reception and signed the contract...with him as co-signer. Those bills followed his credit report around for years under the guise of numerous collection agencies. He took the hit because he refused to pay for anything that happened while he was out in the middle of hell clearing minefields while she was "babysitting" for Dan.

Their story was not unique. The same scenario played out for several of his buddies and numerous guys from other units. The loyalty and respect the young Marines wanted from their women had slipped far below the stories they heard of the Greatest Generation. Women back then knew how to behave like ladies, not skanks.

It wasn't long before Collin received orders to be stationed in Okinawa and Stephanie married Dan, though she didn't completely drop off his radar. Tearful calls of regret in the middle of the night left him wishing that he could drop everything and fly halfway around the world to make her better...to give her the life she wanted. After just one month into his tour in Okinawa, he convinced himself that since they were both so young, and since he deployed so soon after getting engaged, then she wasn't at fault. Just impressionable...a target of manipulation.

Okinawa kept him an ocean away from returning to her. It also helped that women fell all over themselves for him. He used up those girls, tucking them away in his quarters for a month or two before he switched one out for another. A darker hair color, smaller tits, a lazy eye, anything different from the one on her way out...he never got over the constant need for sex. When the tail went from hot to routine, his mind drifted back to Vista, and the flavor of the month was sent packing. There were no offspring, no kids—none that he knew of any-way, and truth be told, he'd know if there was one. Eight-een years of child support on an NCO's salary was top tier for girls looking for that sort of thing.

The other web, the "God, Corps, Country" web, ig-nored his devotion to drinking, which had grown to the point of blacking out on a weekly basis. That web ranked him up and boasted honor for his service. As they should. For Collin eventually sacrificed everything about himself for the Corps.

When he finally got out eight years later, he chose to live, really live. He packed it all up and moved to Las Vegas. If the world was truly going to end on New Year's Eve 1999, he might as well join the party.

c h a p t e r   f i v e

Las Vegas
HALLOWEEN, 2000

A glitter bomb exploded over the dance floor in perfect time with the bass drop and the crowd went apeshit. Collin's arm broke contact with one of the girls he came with, Aimee, as he leaned forward. This wasn't his thing—the club scene, or Halloween—but man was he enjoying it. Like an unapologetic spectator, he was soaking it all in, memorizing it, possible fodder for future fantasies.

Another canon full of glitter burst through the air. That's when the camera in Collin's mind zoomed in and focused on a single, beautiful girl taking center stage on the dance floor. She had a smile so bright that it caused his eyes to soften. She was shaking bits of glitter from her hair as her entire body paid homage to a track being laid down by the DJ.

Aimee rested her elbows on her knees so she could shoulder up to Collin and follow his gaze. They both focused on this woman who moved like the music in the club was coming from inside her. As she rolled her shoulders, one of the spaghetti straps on her silver dress slid down her arm. Without missing a beat, she slid it up and strode off, abruptly ending the show.

"Lauren," Aimee practically shouted in Collin's ear. "What?"

"The girl, the bombshell out there, her name is Lauren James. She's a friend of Tyler and Thom's." Aimee motioned to her over-the-top Vietnamese friend, Thom, and his boyfriend. They were the ones that secured the VIP booth.

Noting the fake smile frozen on Aimee's face, Collin sat back and stretched his arm out over the back of the couch. Even though they weren't on a date, she was the one who had invited him last week to come out on Halloween. They were in the same running group at UNLV and had been friendly for about a month. He didn't have any plans. Besides, she'd assured him that he didn't need to wear a costume, and she alluded to the fact that she'd be in one. One that didn't leave much to the imagination.

"Can I bum a smoke, Collin?" she asked as she cozied back into him.

He smiled as he lit a cigarette and moved it from between his lips to hers. When the cocktail waitress came by, he ordered another round.

Lauren's expression was undiluted joy as she burst into the VIP booth and tumbled into Tyler. She brushed glitter off her palms on the tops of her thighs with a swish, then tossed her head back. Her long hair tickled her face, as it had been doing on the dance floor. She brushed it away and dramatically flopped on Tyler's lap. They both hunched over in a peal of laughter and then he popped her off into the spot next to him. The blonde on the other side of Tyler rolled her eyes at Aimee.

Before Lauren's grand entrance, Collin felt fine not being in costume, but now he suddenly felt out of place in his collared shirt that was tucked into his stiff, belted jeans. He rose to use the bathroom, telling himself to relax as he walked away, but after eight years in the military, that was next to impossible. He basically marched off.

Upon his return, Lauren hopped up to leave and he stepped aside, letting her pass. Her shoulder grazed his as she said, "Excuse me," with a sweet smile. He averted his eyes down to Aimee and kept them there.

Two more scantily clad girls came in as Lauren exited, so Collin and Aimee scooted over to make room. The girls sat and Aimee asked Collin to switch spots. Playing musical chairs had left him pressed up against the partition between their booth and the one next over. And it had just filled up with a bunch of dudes.

"Hey, man!" One of the guys, obviously a tourist, called as he held up a full bottle.

Collin leaned into Aimee. "Do you girls want some company?"

One of the girls shot a glance at the table of guys, now scrambling to see into their area and motioning for them to join in for some drinks. "Ugh…no," she broke off without a moment's hesitation.

Collin shrugged his shoulders to the guys. "Sorry."

"It's okay, man, you want a shot?"

Collin hesitated, wanting to get back in with Aimee on the couch, but she was engrossed with her girlfriends. She didn't bother to introduce him and none of them seemed to care who he was. He pushed himself up over the partition and swung his legs around to slide in with the group of guys.

They howled in victory at his escape. High fives went around the table and shots were poured, downed, and refilled.

"It's his last night as a free man," one told Collin, pointing to his buddy at the center of the group.

"Is he getting married tomorrow?"

"No, he's going into the Army. He ships out to Fort Benning on Monday."

At that declaration, the group of guys went bananas again, whooping and hollering for their friend, the new Private-to-be. Aimee's girlfriends shot the clean-cut guys a round of annoyed expressions topped off with some eye rolling before taking her by the arm and leaving.

"Aww!" one of the guys hollered past Collin. "Nice meeting you!"

Over the next beer, Collin relaxed in his new VIP booth with young guys out looking for a wild night. They made unsuccessful attempts at flirting with some of the other girls who flitted in and out of Thom and Tyler's VIP area. Even though Collin was handsome with an easy-going nature about being totally out of place in Club Utopia, he was still a relic at the age of twenty-eight.

Another thirty minutes passed, and he was ready to roll on out of there.

Until Lauren meandered back up.

Collin's new friends went wild for the fresh meat, while Collin was just happy to see that she was alone.

"Hey, gorgeous!" the ringleader shouted.

Lauren smiled and waved. Her face was angelic.

All the guys except Collin clambered to the partition. "Come here! Join us!" they shouted over each other.

Collin caught her eye as she walked over.

"Hello, yourself," she said.

They made bids for her to climb over the booth—as Collin had done—and join them, but she declined. They laid it on thick, telling her how their buddy had enlisted in the Army and was shipping out Monday.

"Congratulations," she responded with a bright smile. "What an honor."

The future soldier feigned like he had been hit in the heart with an arrow and dramatically fell back, as if shot. They all laughed, except Collin. He couldn't keep his eyes off her.

"Just one shot with us! C'mon…" one of the guys cajoled her as he pulled the glasses together.

There was still half a bottle of vodka on the table and her eyes darted to the top of it and then to the shot glasses. Before she could answer, Collin grabbed the bottle and announced, "I'll pour 'em." Then to Lauren, "Grab a fresh glass from your table."

He poured steep shots into the guys' glasses but covered the top with this thumb as he tipped the bottle over hers. He quickly handed her the empty glass over the partition.

She encompassed the glass so it was hidden in her whole hand and, with a pointed look to Collin, mouthed the words, "thank you."

He winked.

She snapped a group picture of them with one of the guys' cameras but ducked off to the bathroom before responding to the soldier's request for a shot of her alone with him.

Another beer later and with no sign of Aimee or Lauren, Collin decided to call it a night and settle up his bill. $106. Before tip. After clapping the new, young soldier on the back, he hopped back over to the other, now vacant, VIP booth. He looked down upon the dance floor one last time while waiting for the cocktail waitress to run his card. He felt like an anthropologist upon discovery of a lost tribe while leaning over the railing, scanning the crowd for one more glimpse of Lauren. He'd declined a tab of X earlier, but now wished he hadn't. She would have been quite a sight on it. A tap on the shoulder broke his train of thought—$20 to the cocktail waitress and he was out. He didn't bother to hunt Aimee down just to say goodnight.

"Hey!" a silver smear of an angel called over the crunching of boots trekking across the lot outside the nightclub. The scraping noise created by the gravel wearing away at her high heels was slightly out of time with her breathlessness.

Within seconds, Collin found himself face to face with Miss Glitter Bomb herself.

"Damn," she said with an exhale, then with familiarity, she lightly grabbed his arm to steady herself as she pulled a heel across the curb to dislodge a rock from the bottom of her boot. "Twenty bucks to park and they can't bother to pave it."

Collin took her by the other arm and smiled, first taking in her face, then her neckline, then his eyes dipped to the strap that had slipped down her shoulder. Again. He looped his index finger under it and slid it back up.

"I didn't get a chance to properly meet you in there. Or thank you," she said as she stepped back and offered up her hand in a graceful motion. "Lauren James."

Amused, his lips curled up at the corners and his eyes locked onto her face. He hooked his hand under hers and raised it to meet his lips. They softly brushed her knuckles. It was a silly game she was playing, but the vision of her on the dance floor was imprinted in his head. He wanted to play along. So, like a knight from another era, he continued to hold her hand and stepped into her. "Collin St. Germain, pleased to meet you, my dear."

"Not having a good time? Or off to break more hearts elsewhere?"

"I was just getting some air. I'm not much of a heartbreaker, ma'am."

"Want to go for a walk? Or we could go back in and take in some more asinine extravagance?" Lauren challenged him with a teasing smile.

"Are you sure there's not someone else in there waiting to take you for a walk?"

"What, like a boyfriend?" she half snorted. "Puhleese, just give me a second to run and get my coat." Lauren caught herself before she trampled back across the rocky lot and switched gears to the dirt walkway, covering it in a girlish skip.

Collin lit a cigarette and waited.

Moments later, she re-emerged, wrapped up tightly in a fitted black coat. Gliding over the walkway with more confidence now, the sway of her hips rocked the hem of the coat back and forth like a rolling wave.

Collin flipped the butt of his cigarette away and extended his arm in a chivalrous fashion so she could hook into the crook of his elbow. They fell in step.

"Where shall we go?"

"Let's walk toward the fountains," he answered and led the way to Bellagio.

"That's a long way and they don't run all night."

"We could stop and have a drink if we don't feel like going all the way down. A drink made by an actual bartender."

"Fair enough." They made their way north on the Strip. "Do you go to UNLV?" Lauren asked.

"Yeah, I'm an engineering major. I'm trying to get through it in three years though, before my GI money runs out."

"GI money? Is that a…a scholarship? Or a grant?"

"No." His tone wasn't patronizing, but he chuckled under his breath. "GI Bill, it's the money Uncle Sam pays toward college for your service."

"So, you were in the Army?"

"Marines. I got out two years ago and traveled around some before deciding to go for a higher education." He smirked before he continued. "I joined up when I was barely out of high school and less than a year out of boot camp, I deployed to the Gulf for Desert Storm."

"That guy in there, hopefully he won't have a war to go off to. I don't know anyone who's ever been to war. How long were you there? In the Gulf, I mean."

"Not quite a year. Why don't you tell me where you're from?"

"Nowhere very interesting, Minneapolis, I was raised by my grandmother's half-sister and started dance training at the ripe old age of thirteen, too late in life for a real career. That's my life in a nutshell. The guy, Tyler, Thom's boyfriend, he grew up next door, but he escaped first because he's a few years ahead of me in school."

When Collin asked her why she moved from Minneapolis to Las Vegas, her smile faltered briefly, then she smoothed it over with a laugh and an overly cheery, "Oh my God, Collin, have you ever been there in the winter?" Without a beat, she moved the conversation back to him. "What's it like to go from being a Marine to being a student? Like with teachers? Isn't that frustrating for you?"

Collin knew what she was up to. "It's not so bad. When do you graduate?"

Lauren sighed. "I'm shooting for two more years, like the spring of 2002."

"And then?"

"Hopefully I'll move out of Tyler's guest room. What about you? When do you graduate?"

"In a year, December of 2001. I don't care if I walk, though."

"Do you think you'd go back into the service?"

"No, I've had enough."

"Like hitting rock bottom enough? Or just ready for a change enough?"

"Rock bottom enough, yeah. My last two years in Okinawa were a foggy haze—the daily grind bled into the nightly trips to the bar. Keeping the 'For God, Corps, Country' mentality twenty-four/seven doesn't allow for much personal growth either, if there is such a thing.... It's easier to fake being satisfied with the life inside, rather than admitting any desire for a life outside the Corps. So, you just numb the desire away by drinking, all the time. I still like my Maker's Mark, but not a bottle a night." He looked over at her. "Most nights anyway."

"Did you have to stay in for so long?"

"No...yes...there was nowhere else for me to go. After the four years, it was just easier to keep on with the familiar. Then it was Okinawa, different location, same routine, but I had to grow up there. It was a crash course in how the world really works. It would've only been a matter of time before a different kind of web would've imprisoned me. There's plenty of women ready to poke holes in their diaphragms in hopes of getting a piece of a Marine's salary for eighteen years. Luckily no one ever caught me. But the web that did catch me, the one that kept me entangled, just ignored my devotion to drinking and ranked me up."

She nodded.

He whistled a "sheesh" and lightened his tone. "Okinawa, it's an island south of Japan. Eight years, that has a nice even ring to it, don't you think? Fortunately, I was able to get my shit together enough to dry out and fantasize about life on the outside."

They walked along in silence for almost a block until Collin asked, "How comfortable are those boots to walk in?"

"This would be the perfect place to stop." They entered the newly remodeled Desert Passage Shops of the Aladdin.

Once situated at an empty bar under a moving sky that suspended the perception of time, he helped Lauren with her coat. She excused herself to the bathroom and he flagged down the bartender while admiring her exposed sparkling skin as she walked away.

Collin ordered them two Maker's, hers with Coke. As the bartender poured his neat, Collin cleared his throat.

"Double?" the bartender asked without missing a beat.

Collin gave him a curt nod and placed his credit card down.

"Keep it open, buddy," Collin said and took a huge gulp, resetting the level in his glass to a straight single pour.

Collin pushed the drink toward Lauren when she returned. She took a small sip. The instant heat that flushed her face told him that she wasn't a drinker, perhaps not even twenty-one.

"Is this what it looked like when you were in the Gulf?" she asked and they both turned to look at the brightly colored awnings draped off the minaret façades. Display windows with trendy fashions juxtaposed the mosaic covered walls on either side of the man-made stream snaking through the arcade. The faux sky was beginning to turn from twilight to dusk.

"This place looks like you could find a magic carpet for the right price," Collin said with a chuckle. He finished his drink, which was replaced before he set the glass down. "The Saudi desert is a sand pit. The only thing I'd ever want you to experience there is a night under the stars, that's something to behold. Definitely, not—" he looked up to the faux stars making their way across the projected sky "—not this." He took a sip and held her gaze, charming her with his mysterious past.

"Tell me more about the dance piece you and Tyler are working on."

"Tyler's a grad student, I told you that, right? And I'm an undergrad majoring in dance. He's working on his final presentation and uses dancers, us, in the undergrad program to perform his choreography. His repertoire is extremely sophisticated and showcases transcendental dance inspired by far Eastern religious practices, specifically yoga. The inspiration came to him during a Hatha yoga class when he thought of the asanas—those are yoga poses—as building blocks for dances. He began stringing yoga poses together to use in choreography. He told me that he had this vision of us all 'performing yoga' for the masses."

Collin nodded, but then his eyes quickly dropped down to get another look at her breasts that begged to be tamed within a bra. "What color are your eyes? I couldn't make them out in the club and they seem to change from blue to grey in here, but maybe it's just the sky."

"Blue, well, almost grey sometimes. Unless I'm wearing blue, then dark blue. Why do you ask?"

The bartender suddenly appeared. "Would you like something instead of this?" He pointed to her Maker's and Coke.

"No." She looked back to Collin.

"I wonder what they would look like if you wore a blue top. Don't take this the wrong way, but your dress is so low cut, that the only contrast for your eyes is your skin. They can't pop. But if you wore a sapphire top, maybe something silky, that covered more of your chest, your eyes would sparkle."

Lauren's face couldn't mask the smack it felt, the shame it endured, or the itch her hand had to throw her drink in his face. But it was the tear that threatened to fall from the corner of her eye that made him regret saying it.

"All I'm saying is that you are a really pretty…beautiful…girl, Lauren." He put his hand over hers and felt it jerk slightly. "You don't need to cheapen yourself to get attention. Sorry, I didn't mean to hurt your feelings."

The tear streaked down her cheek and she rubbed her chin over her shoulder to keep it from dripping. She pulled her hand out from under his and slumped back in her chair. "It's Halloween, everybody dresses like this." Her voice was husky.

He didn't want her to start crying at the bar. "You're right. I didn't even think of that." He opened his arms and presented himself to her in a self-deprecating way. "Obviously, right? Halloween…not on my radar."

It worked, she laughed and took a deep breath.

She slid her arms back in her coat and awkwardly pulled it up over her shoulders.

After that rough moment, Collin questioned if he had been too harsh on her. He was pleasantly surprised how she rallied and switched topics by asking more questions about his military service. She wanted to know what the guy from the club would be in for on Monday morning when he left for boot camp. Collin told her about his first day of boot camp and then paid for the drinks. She was enrapt.

Early morning joggers were beginning to replace the "walk of shame" honorees on the sidewalk as the pair started back to the club. Collin slid his arm around her to guide them through the foot traffic and she leaned into him. Glitter dusted his shoulder when her head dropped down with a sigh. His nose sought out the top of her head and he resisted the urge to pull her in closer. She was bundled up and soft under his arm.

When they finally stopped in front of the club, Collin brushed the overgrown locks of streaked blonde hair to the side and angled her face up. Her eyes were heavy.

She rose onto her toes as he debated whether to kiss her.

"What do you say, Miss James? We could get together again? Get through this week's classes and go blow off some steam Friday night?" He decided that it could wait until he saw her again.

"I think I'm free this Friday. What did you have in mind?" Her rib cage shifted, trying to get him to capture it in his hand. He was immune to her antics, though, and didn't take the bait.

"Well, I already know you're one helluva dancer, so how 'bout I take you dancing?"

"Dancing?" She snapped out of her trance and stepped back.

"Maybe not here, no costume required."

Lauren shifted from one foot to the other and crossed her arms over her chest. Her feet must have been killing her.

After a moment, she brightly mustered, "Fine. Where should I meet you?"

"I can pick you up."

"Let's just meet at Moose's, by UNLV. Do you know it? Ten?"

"Yes. Twenty-two hundred hours, ma'am, Friday at Moose's. Roger that. You're a smart cookie not giving your address out to a strange man."

"I know, 'til Friday then, Staff Sergeant."

"Looking forward to it, Miss James." He saluted her.

She blew him a kiss and went back into the club to find her ride.

c h a p t e r   s i x

Collin had ventured to the east end of campus only once before when he first arrived at UNLV. None of his classes were down there, but the Alta Ham Fine Arts Center (HFA) was. Instead of going to the Student Center to study the Wednesday before their date, he found an alcove overlooking the HFA dance studio entrance.

An hour went by as he watched dancers go in and out. Some hung out in the grassy area in front of the building. They appeared confident, using their backpacks or each other as pillows under the trees, taking long neck rolls while talking, all the while scanning the bodies of every passerby.

Collin was fascinated by this culture he'd never considered. Their hair was disheveled in top knots, bare faces, and they donned mismatched layers of tights and spandex covered by ratty t-shirts that fell from their shoulders. They were enchanting and, surprisingly, very intimidating creatures.

He was about to leave when Lauren finally arrived, rushing up the sidewalk. She stood out in a white oxford that was untucked from her black pants. The flap on her backpack flopped around and its contents threatened to fall out at any moment. She unbuttoned her cuffs as she ran and ignored the swans peering her way. Her chest heaved as she stopped short to pull open the heavy door and dart in, obviously late for class. Collin's attention went back to the lounging dancers; they were already back to their discussion.

A round of dance classes must have started in the HFA because the crowd thinned considerably in front of the building. Collin walked up the same path Lauren had run down when something caught his eye on the sidewalk. He reached down to pick it up; it was a name tag from Mimi's Café with her name on it.

chapter seven

Las Vegas
NOVEMBER 4, 2000

Collin detested being late, especially for a first date. Right before he left, the phone rang and stupidly, he answered it thinking it might be Lauren. Not possible. She didn't have his number. It was Mayhem's sister, Donna, who happened to be Stephanie's best friend. They were all partying together, and since they were three hours ahead of him, they were also ahead by that many more hours of drinking. The phone on their end was passed around at a house party back home so Mayhem could say hi, then it was some other guys Collin knew, then some he didn't, then…Stephanie…who tried to act like she didn't care. He didn't want to be rude, but he was going to be late meeting Lauren. Finally, he maneuvered out of an obnoxious conversation where he ended up on speaker. He flew out the door reminding himself to get caller ID.

She wasn't anywhere to be found in Moose's. Feeling edgy and irritated, he left, figuring he'd just go get a bottle and take it home. But then, he spotted her leaning against the passenger door of his truck. A smile spread over his face as he shot across the parking lot, closing the space between them with urgency.

"Lauren," he exclaimed as he clasped her hand; it was freezing. "I'm sorry, I was running late and I don't have your number. I guess we forgot that part last week."

She didn't respond, but she didn't pull her hand back either. She tilted her head to one side and took him in for a moment. His hair was slicked back in a neat way that shone under the street lamp. He'd just shaved that evening; she could have inspected his face with her palm and not feel the slightest bit of stubble.

He tugged on her hand and sweetly rocked her. "Forgive me?"

She cocked an eyebrow and stepped aside for him to open the door.

He guided her arm as she hoisted herself up on the side rail to enter the lifted truck. The "spic and span" interior gave off a whiff of Armor All that he hoped would impress her.

"You didn't think I'd stand you up, did you?" Collin reached over to take her hands and rub them between his. He moved them in front of the vent once it started to blow warm air. "Better?"

She nodded.

He looked over his shoulder to back out and opened his right arm to clasp the back of her seat. His hand deliberately brushed her shoulder before he reached down to shift into first.

"How were your classes this week?" he asked.

"Good, for the most part. How about yours? Have you had a good week?"

Her habit of turning the conversation back to him was even more noticeable than the night they first met.

"Time went by exceptionally slow for me this week." He glanced over.

She caught his eye and smiled that same bright smile he remembered from the club. He'd finally pierced the cold front she'd put up. "Okay, I have to admit, I've been checking the clock a little more than usual this week, too, Collin." The volume in her voice had picked back up to normal and she shifted in her seat to face him. "So, where are we going?"

"It's a surprise."

"I love surprises."

They pulled up to The Country Star Restaurant by Monte Carlo and if she had any apprehension about country line dancing, she hid it well.

"Are you game for a real honky-tonk night complete with buckets of beer, darlin'?" he asked in a seductive drawl.

"You'll have to teach me some moves," she flirted back as they stepped up to the coat check girl.

He helped get her coat off and when she turned back to him, he paused in a moment of tenderness for this young girl. She wore a teal blue blouse with a cowl neck that skimmed her waist and a slim-fitting black pair of jeans. Her collarbone and shoulders were on muted display, and when she glanced up at him in a hopeful way, her eyes caught the color of her top.

"You look stunning," he gasped.

By the end of her second beer, she'd loosened up and was at as much ease in this type of club as she was in the one where they met last weekend. Collin taught her some line dance moves on the spot; of course, she easily picked them up. As the night wore on, he pulled her in close to his chest with a firm grip on her low back. She offered no resistance.

The hours and buckets of beer resulted in constant trips to the ladies' room, though. He surmised that she wasn't much of a drinker when she'd become wobbly on her feet after only four light beers.

It was well past 2:00 a.m. when she came out of the bathroom for what seemed like the hundredth time that night. Collin had her jacket over his arm. "Let's go," he suggested and wrapped her up.

His pace was slow as they made their way to his truck, causing Lauren to creep in closer under his arm for warmth. No matter how deep into the fold she was, she continued to shiver.

"Cold?" he asked.

"Nervous," came out of her mouth quickly. She jerked her head back away from his shoulder. "I mean…I don't know why I said that. I'm just cold." She forced a half-laugh.

God, she is still so young.

Lauren's shoulders dropped down and away from her ears as she visibly relaxed when the heat infiltrated the cabin during the drive back to her place. Collin cracked his window to smoke. They didn't talk, but he stole a few glances her way. Once she looked over at the same time and they smiled at each other. An easy, comfortable smile. He sealed the window back up when he finished his cigarette. She pointed out her house and he drove a couple blocks past it to grant them some anonymity for a little while longer. Collin shifted to neutral and lifted the parking brake. The click of his seat belt releasing punctuated the silence in a promise of movement within the confined space between them. He reached over and pressed the button to unclick hers as well and when he sat back, she guided the strap away from her.

She deliberately turned to face him. "I had a good time."

"I know."

Lauren's face was already in position for his lips to land on hers.

It was such a natural kiss that Collin didn't even recall leaning in for it. Lauren's mouth parted, and with a practiced skill, he kissed her in the way a man does that causes a woman to wilt.

Collin held back, though; he was a more seasoned lover and knew that he could've taken her much farther than just two high school kids making out in a car. He limited his hands to caressing her upper shoulders, nothing lower. At first, her hand was still—palm down—resting on top of his thigh. But within moments, her fingertips began grazing his knee.

Suddenly, there was a knock on the window.

Collin and Lauren abruptly pulled away from each other at the unwelcome intrusion. It was Aimee and her friend, Thom, making the motion for him to roll down the window. Aimee sheepishly stood a few feet back. Collin exhaled in irritation and pressed the power window button from his door.

"What, Thom? Jesus!" Lauren demanded.

Collin gave Aimee a friendly wave.

She peeked her head over Thom's shoulder. "Hey, Collin."

Thom addressed Lauren. "Tyler wants you to come in. C'mon." His voice rang a little bossy as he held his ground with no intention of leaving Lauren in the truck.

Collin appreciated that these guys were looking out for her even though he would've liked just a little more time with her. "Go on," he encouraged, "you should go inside and get some rest."

A fiery look came over her face as she yanked up her coat. "Yes, it must be past my bedtime," she huffed and got out of the car.

Collin stifled a laugh. She was so very cute. He understood why she was pissed, but she'd see him again. "Good night," he called to the three of them and pulled away. A quick check in the rearview mirror verified that she'd turned back to watch him go.

Collin came by the next day with some flowers, but she wasn't home.

"She's at work," Tyler told him as he put the lilies in a vase. "She'll love these."

c h a p t e r   e i g h t

Mimi's Café
HOLIDAY BREAK, 2000

"I'm not trying to be a dick," Collin began, "but seriously, how do you get a D in Ballet?"

"Attendance."

Collin set her grades down on the table. "And the C- in Choreography?"

"Same."

Lauren was working a double on the first Saturday of winter break, so Collin had come up to have lunch with her between shifts. Most of the staff left town for the holiday, so she volunteered to work overtime through New Year's Eve. A female server walked over to the booth designated for servers in the back of Mimi's with her cash-out slip.

"Can you sign me out?" she asked Lauren.

"Is there anymore silverware in back?"

"Nope."

Lauren scribbled on the girl's pad. "Are you done for the rest of 2000?"

"Yeah, guess I won't see you 'til next year!"

Both girls laughed and Lauren got up to hug the other server. "Bye!" Her back was to Collin as she watched the girl go and he wondered if her face was wistful.

Lauren flopped back down in the booth and looked across the table with a smile. "Do you want to hang out when I get off tonight?"

"Why don't you quit working and get some financial aid? At this rate, you'll end up flunking out."

"Because, well I told you, my guardian growing up was my great-aunt...half-aunt...she's part of an Inuit tribe really far north in Canada. When I tried to apply for financial aid, she was getting her rights to a piece of land there reinstated. Canada took the land from them and called it the Northwest Territories, but then they had to give it back and she was entitled to some property on this island, Baffin Island. Anyway, long story longer, her status as my guardian and *that* whole ordeal made applying for financial aid next to impossible for me. But...UNLV has a contingency—if you work full-time, even in the service industry, you get in-state tuition immediately, which is like, fifty-six dollars a credit. So, that's what I did when I moved here. And voilà," she

spread her arms over the rack of silverware she was pol-
ishing. "My rollups are paying for my degree."

"And, exactly, what are you going to do with this
dance degree?"

Lauren pulled her hands through her hair and adjusted her ponytail. The bags under her eyes were prom-
inent today. "I don't know, Collin. I barely have time to
figure out what I'm going to do tomorrow."

Collin tapped his lighter on the table and studied her
as she started back up on rolling silverware. She was
bright, sometimes overexcited, but that was her youth.
She liked to ask a lot of questions. "Have you ever
thought about changing majors?"

She shrugged.

Collin reached over for a stack of linen and a handful
of silver. As he began helping her with the rollups, he
offered, "I'd pay for you to take one of those assess-
ments that determines what you'd be good at. Maybe
you'd get some ideas about a new major."

"Okay."

"I'd also love to take you on a date to the financial
aid office. We could do paperwork together, you could
apply for yourself, not as a dependent...." He glanced
up and saw her smiling, even though she was pretending
to concentrate on her task. "We could type in your social
security number a million times into a computer...."

She giggled.

"We could even…gasp…make copies of your W-2s and submit them!"

She beamed. "Can we get ice cream after?"

"We can get anything you want."

"Good, 'cause if I switch majors, I plan on eating ice cream whenever the hell I want."

chapter nine

Collin's Place
JANUARY 5, 2001

When Collin checked the mail Friday afternoon, he was surprised to find a letter from his dad. The news that his father, Claude St. Germain, had officially left his mother for good added insult to the injury of his hangover.

Why Tyler and Thom thought that taking Lauren on a pub crawl for her twenty-first birthday last night was a good idea was beyond him. At least the dry heaving had ceased a couple hours ago, and he had tucked her into bed to sleep it off.

With a strong pot of coffee and a smoke, he sat out back to read the letter. It reiterated the same thing he'd been telling his son for decades now: all St. Germain men are cursed. And women were just the beginning of it. Collin's father and mother had been at odds for years, and now that both of his younger sisters were out of the house, there was no longer any reason to stay together. Collin didn't want to imagine what the final blow-out fight was like. Any speculation on his part would make him lose his mind and his temper—equally directed to his father and mother both.

In addition to the letter, there was an article from *Fortean Times Magazine* in the envelope that had a sticky note under the title with his dad's shaky handwriting on it. *Never wish for anything, son.*

Collin sighed as he peeled it off. "Here we go again," he muttered to himself.

"Minefields of Deadly Wishes"

The endless miles of desert make for a near-impossible playing field when it comes to the game of war, forcing the US to become innovative with its strategic tactics while moving toward Kuwait City. However, a new theory insinuates that the Iraqis do not rely on new ideas, but rather old traditions. Ancient traditions.

Recent interviews suggest that Sadaam Hussein's inner circle made contact with the supernatural, the djinn, to obtain US intelligence that wouldn't have been available to the Iraqis in any other manner. Folklore suggests that this is nothing new and that the djinn have been advising leaders in the Middle East for centuries. Westerners know djinn as "genies" who often grant wishes – usually with superfluous outcomes that bring only bad luck to the wish makers.

The source, whose identity has been protected for his safety, witnessed a red djinni – one who claimed to be the leader of the red djinn—appear before one of Saddam's top advisors on several occasions. During these appearances, the djinni being would give the exact locations and routes proposed by the multiple USMC Task Forces, poised near the Kuwait border just days before the Liberation of Kuwait. The source also claims that the red djinni advised Saddam where to place his minefields in the desert to create the maximum number of US causalities. When asked if this djinni being had a specific name, it was reported that the source paled and would not speak it out loud for fear of invoking IT back into his presence.

Obviously, this claim that the Iraqis had access to the US's planned route into Kuwait City has been analyzed and debunked, because *if* Sadaam had the route, *why* didn't he intercept US forces with the full force of the Iraqi army? *Or perhaps*—and this is just theory—perhaps, there was a last-minute change of plans.

The Iraqis weren't the only ones using unconventional forces in Desert Storm. The US has relied on contractors to support their armed forces since the Revolutionary War, and the Gulf War brought contractor involvement to a whole new level.

For dealing with hidden minefields in the desert during the Gulf War, the US military employs a technology called the "line charge," or more formally, a Mine Clearing Line Charge (MCLC). Essentially, a line charge is a 400-foot rope with blocks of C4 explosive spread evenly along its length. The rope is coiled into a bin, attached to a sidewinder missile, and deployed across a live mine field.

Prior to the Gulf War, the time to prep additional line charges would take up to ten minutes, allowing for significant exposure in the field. In the early months of Desert Storm, the Marine Corps quietly purchased a system from Northrup Grumman, which allowed three complete line charges to be placed in the back of a single AAV. This allowed the lead vehicle to continue to move forward without the need to stop and reset between each shot.

This new technology proved successful on February 24, 1991, when the Marines used the three-shot line charge to quickly clear a path to Kuwait City. The swiftness at which minefields could be rendered inert allowed follow-on forces safe passage behind the lead AAV.

It was later discovered that the Iraqi Army had heavily fortified a far different area of the Kuwaiti desert. Either the Marines had excellent intelligence or perhaps a more sinister deception was played out against Saddam Hussein. *Be careful what you wish for....*

PART II

chapter ten

Las Vegas
FEBRUARY 9, 2001

She tapped her foot under the table as Collin unloaded two cases of beer into the fridge. There was still an hour before they needed to get to the airport to pick up Mayhem and his sister, Donna. Lauren was unsure if she was staying at his place for the weekend or not. It not, it would be the first one since Christmas.

"So, you think they'll be up for the party tomorrow night? Should I bring my costume here or, uh, get ready at...."

Home? Tyler's? Somewhere else?

"I thought you brought it over here."

"Well, it's in my dance bag."

There were two beers in his hands when he turned to face her. He smiled when she reached for one. "You really are nervous. He's going to like you."

She choked on the flow of beer that took her throat by surprise, which in turn, caused her eyes to water.

"Easy there, Lauren. Don't worry, Donna's a sweetheart and lots of fun. You two'll get along great."

"Do you want me to stay here this weekend or not?" she blurted out.

"What?" He looked genuinely surprised by the question. "Is that what you're all spun up about?"

She shrugged with her hands up and nodded.

"Why wouldn't you stay here this weekend?"

"I just...." She took a breath and gathered her thoughts. "I guess I was worried that Stephanie might be coming with them."

He came around the counter and sat down at the barstool next to her. His hands found hers clasped tightly in her lap. He massaged them into surrender. "I haven't seen or spoken to her in years. And I have no desire to ever do so again, trust me." His eyes bore into hers, not allowing her gaze to escape and shift down. "Donna won't bring her up, not to you, or to me. Stephanie isn't a factor in this weekend or my life."

Her forehead dove into his chest with a muffled, "Sorry, I'm just being paranoid."

He pulled her up by the shoulders. "Finish your beer and have another. There's nothing to worry about, we're going to light it up this weekend. You'll see."

She obeyed as he hopped up and headed toward the living room.

"And unpack all your stuff, babe!" he called from the other room. His head popped back into the kitchen to regard her in a serious manner. "You belong here. You can bring all your clothes and all your stuff over. Put 'em wherever you want, move things around."

She tossed the beer can into the trash and wasted no time opening another. "Do you think Donna might need to borrow something to wear for the party?"

He grinned. "Naw, she'll be all right. I told them to step it up. It's Tyler and Thom's shindig, after all. They'll like her."

Lauren wasn't so sure about that, but she didn't respond. Instead, she splashed some cold water on her face, touched up her lipstick, and donned a confident smile to keep for the rest of the weekend.

As one might expect, any and all current and/or former Marines would be first in line to attend a Pimps-n-Hos themed birthday party for a hot twenty-something on a Saturday night in Las Vegas. Mayhem was quick to express his enthusiasm for the invite to Aimee's birthday party less than a second after Collin told him about it on the phone. At first, Lauren was apprehensive to bring Collin's buddy and his sister *(Stephanie's closest friend...ugh!)* to such a skin-filled show of debauchery; she wanted to make a good impression. But after seeing a few photos from Okinawa, she realized that Mayhem would probably like her even better than if they declined.

While the four of them were getting ready for the party, Donna emerged from the guest bathroom wearing a black, latex skirt so tiny that the crotch of her sequined G-string was visible when she sat. On top was a red bustier with black lacing and matching spiked cuffs wrapped tightly around each wrist. The piece de resistance was a tassel whip that she used to playfully smack her own thigh in response to seeing Lauren's eyes widen.

"My sister, always the wallflower," Mayhem chastised.

A wolf whistle came from Collin, immediately causing Lauren to reevaluate her own costume choice.

Lauren wore an oversized, button-down, men's shirt in white without cufflinks so that her fingertips peeked out from the sleeves. One of Collin's neckties hung in a loose knot from the collar, allowing for a modest opening to expose her neck and chest. She had on a bra and boy shorts under it, neither visible, though. There may have been an old pair of black thigh high boots buried in her closet at Tyler's. She wished she'd have thought to bring them. She could have fastened them with a safety pin, making this *Pretty Woman* costume more obvious. At the time, wearing tube socks instead of shoes seemed like a cute idea, but now she wished for a pair of heels.

"At least I can dance all night without my feet hurting," she muttered to herself as she sprayed the last of the temporary red dye on her hair.

There were a couple rounds of shots before the four of them left and plenty more to be had at the party.

Collin was right, both Mayhem and Donna had a blast. Aimee was in her glory as queen ho, with a tiara to boot. Even though it was Lauren's circle of friends, she was having a hard time acting normal. It wasn't too late in the evening before her nerves and the shots caught up with her. She shrunk back toward the kitchen, away from the large, boisterous group gathered around Donna. Collin was laughing harder than she'd ever seen him before as Donna's sharp tongue entertained the gays.

Mayhem appeared next to her under the kitchen light, his smile was easy and his eyes sympathetic. "You okay, Lauren?" He took a hold of her upper arm and steadied her.

She nodded in exaggeration, worried that if she opened her mouth, she'd either slur something completely unintelligible or throw up all over him.

"C'mon, honey, let's get some fresh air."

As she sat hunched over on the curb, Mayhem produced a bottle of water. "Here, take a sip. Been trying to keep up with Donna all night, huh?"

She peeked up through her clumpy mess of hair to find him looking down on her with brotherly concern.

"Don't worry about her. They've known each other since she was a kid. He's always been someone's boyfriend to her. And partner in crime to her torturous older bro."

"Stephanie...." Lauren croaked.

"They're cut from the same cloth, my sis and her. Don't worry, Donna isn't whispering about times gone by in Grover's ear."

Lauren moaned and the fast appearing sweat prior to vomiting commenced.

"All right, young lady, let's get you up. I'll hold your hair back."

Three Months Later

"When's your last final?" Tyler asked after taking a seat across the table from Lauren.

She'd been studying for it at Café Copioh for the past few hours and barely glanced up when he joined her. "Hold on one sec," she mumbled as she reached for the highlighter resting against the side of her book. "Let me mark my spot." After a yellow sweep across a line in her textbook, her head popped up, and she stretched toward the ceiling. "In about thirty minutes."

Before she could continue, the barista stopped at the table. "Dry capp, skim milk?" He set down an immaculately swirled cappuccino in front of Lauren. The foam had a heart in it.

She pointed to her empty cup. "I already got mine."

"Oh?" he asked, mocking innocence. He smelled like cloves and patchouli. "I thought you might like a second one. You've been going at it for almost two hours now."

A pinkish flush stained her cheeks. "Thank you…yeah…it's a final."

"What class?"

She flashed the cover of her textbook to the barista. "Criminal Justice." Reclaiming her composure, she tilted her head and absently began twirling a lock of hair around her finger. "Are you taking classes this semester?"

He set the empty mug back down and placed both palms on the table comfortably; the unmistakable stance of someone ready to start in on a long conversation.

"You're going to be late," Tyler snapped at Lauren.

The barista's eyes danced with humor and he backed off. "See you later, Lauri."

She couldn't recall his name and a quick glance at his nametag didn't help. It had masking tape over it displaying CUPPAJOE written with a sharpie. She closed her book and looked back to Tyler, dismissing the barista for good.

The empty cup remained on the table as he sauntered back over to the counter.

"What's the latest on the studio in LA?" she directed to Tyler.

He drew a cigarette out of the pack in his jacket and fidgeted with it while catching her up on the business venture. "My portfolio was picked up by an independent choreographer who's looking to break into the yoga business. We think there's a market for a yoga studio that focuses on the outer beauty of the practice. If that's going to work anywhere, L.A. would be the place."

"Yoga as a physical practice only? It wouldn't be yoga, it'd be 'poga,' " she joked as she stood and collected her things. "Thom always gets his way with you, doesn't he?"

Tyler abruptly released his cigarette and rocked back in his chair with a groan. "Two weeks."

She snatched up the remains from his cigarette and deposited them in the empty cup. "It's worth it, even if it's just to get him off your back."

"I'll walk you to class."

Lauren dropped a couple bucks on the table without looking back to the barista.

"You're too nice," Tyler observed and opened the door for her. As they walked across the parking lot, they joked around with silly names for this *yoga-meets-modeling-meets-the-screen* idea of Tyler's until he switched topics.

"When's the last time you've been home? Your room's collecting dust."

"I came by last week," she responded airily.

"We've got to get everything out by the end of May."

"How about right after graduation. We're still going out to lunch after you walk, right? We just come over after."

"Sure."

"Sure, pure, yoga?"

"It's not a Dr. Seuss book."

"How about 'Pura Yoga?' "

Tyler cocked an eyebrow.

chapter eleven

Las Vegas
MAY 2001

Helping people move was never one of Collin's favorite pastimes, yet he always ended up on top of everyone's list when the time came. The night after UNLV's graduation ceremony for the class of 2001, he found himself loading the last of Tyler and Thom's boxes while they meticulously finished packing up their kitchen. Earlier in the day, Collin hauled off two recliners to Goodwill. He'd hoped that was the last of his obligations, but Lauren was slow about collecting her things from the guest bedroom.

Late into the evening, Thom and Tyler were still debating if they should buy a new desk or take the old one. Collin went upstairs to check on her.

"You haven't worn any of those clothes for at least six months," he observed when he found her pulling stuff out of the donation bag she'd tied up earlier.

Her head snapped up like she had just been caught with her hand in the cookie jar. In a brisk move, she dropped the bag, and bent down to pick up the clothes littering the floor. "I know, I just wanted to make sure there wasn't anything in there that I might need for the summer." She clumsily retied the bag and brushed her hands together.

Collin picked up that and two other bags; only a suitcase and a boombox remained. "I think we're done. They're fussing over a desk."

Lauren turned slowly to take in the room. "I guess it's time to say goodbye." She hoisted up the suitcase and paused. "Tyler was really good to me, letting me stay here and all. Thanks for helping them today."

Collin motioned to the boombox. "I can take that, too. Now let's get out of here before I end up rearranging the back of the U-Haul for a desk."

He was relieved that she wasn't weepy to see off her best friend. She made a stop to the bathroom and Tyler pulled the boombox from his hand. At the truck, Tyler waited until he unloaded all her bags in the back before handing him the boombox.

"Thanks," Collin said as he placed it on top of the bags.

"Thank you," Tyler enunciated the two words as he firmly shook Collin's hand. His confident hand shake gave Collin pause as it seemed out of place for an openly gay man.

Collin lit a cigarette and leaned against the bed of the truck. "You don't need to worry about her. She's a good girl and I'll take care of her."

Tyler inhaled deeply.

"You want a drag?" Collin offered.

Tyler shook his head. "Thanks, though. You two should come visit us in Cali."

Lauren called a "Goodbye" back into the house and scurried over to the truck. "Thom needs you."

It wasn't long before summer school began and the desert heat kept them sequestered inside. Collin had been keeping tabs on her studies during the previous semester, but that stopped over the summer. She was constantly writing papers, reading, and completing her projects on time.

As June turned to July, the habits of being a couple surfaced and repeated. They ordered Thai food every Friday night and ate it from to-go boxes wearing pajamas in front of the TV. Collin drove her to campus every morning except Wednesdays when she went to yoga before her first class. They went to Sam's Club on Sundays.

It was the first Sunday of July when their relationship shifted into unchartered territory. Just prior to that moment, Lauren had hustled into the house carrying a huge package of paper towels, leaving Collin to lug in everything else.

"Let the machine get it!" he hollered, but she was already inside. He loaded the bulk of their purchases in both hands.

Irritated that she didn't bother to come back and open the door for him, he finagled it open. First to the laundry room to drop off the detergent, then into the kitchen to find out who was on the phone. He was going to give her a hard time if the machine beat her—just a little ribbing, nothing too serious.

Her back was to him and the paper towel pack was at her feet. "When?"

He set the stuff on the counter and froze.

"Oh, my God," she sighed and leaned over the sink like she was going to vomit. "How come you didn't let me know sooner?"

Whatever the person on the other end said set her off.

"That's the day after tomorrow! The day right before the fourth. Do you know how impossible it will be to get a flight? If you would've done the right thing and called me last week when you knew he was going downhill, I could have been there! I could've...." Her faced turned away from the phone and she tucked her nose into the crook of her arm to stifle a sob.

Collin came up behind her and circled his arms around her waist. She turned into him and buried her face in his shoulder. He eased the phone out of her hand and lifted it to his ear. "Who is this?"

It was her mother calling to inform her daughter that her father lost his battle with pancreatic cancer. It was the first-time Collin had ever spoken to Lauren's mom and it was no surprise that she didn't know who he was or that they lived together.

"I just thought she should know," Connie admitted once he explained that this was his number, not Tyler's new one. "It shouldn't make a difference in her life, our lives. I bet it's been over ten years since he's seen her."

"It's been almost twenty," he corrected. Recently, Lauren confided in him that her dad had walked out on her and Connie before she turned two. She couldn't even recall the last time they spoke on the phone, guessing that it was before she moved to Vegas. "When's the funeral?"

Lauren's tear-stained face pulled away from his chest and said, "Wednesday," before her mother responded.

"Do you want to go?" he asked, not caring if Connie was still on the line.

She shook her head as her mother rattled off a list of all the reasons why she shouldn't go. Collin cut her off with, "I'm going to hang up now. Connie, you're always welcome to come visit us down here if you like. Good-bye."

"She won't."

"I know, but it was the easiest way to end the conversation."

She bent down to pick up the paper towels and chucked them on the counter. "I don't even fucking know how I feel right now, let alone what to do."

At least a half a dozen things to say dropped into his head, but none were true. Her dad didn't lead a good life. He never expressed any remorse for abandoning her. All those things would make Lauren feel guilty for not contacting him before he died.

Still, losing her dad.

"Let's go lie down," he suggested once the paper towels had been stowed away. "Take a nap?"

She nodded and allowed him to lead her upstairs. After slipping off her shoes, she crawled in next to him. He let her cry it out on his chest without commenting.

He woke up first. Shadows of the open blinds made horizontal stripes across the wall. He wiggled his arm out from under her head and got up to shut them. His right hand tingled with pins and needles, so he used his left one to turn on the lamp. When he awkwardly bumped the shade, she woke.

"What time is it?"

"Seven, maybe eight." He moved to the edge of the bed and stroked her shoulder. "I was thinking we could drive up to Mount Charleston this weekend. Maybe leave Thursday?"

"To stay at the lodge up there?"

"No, to camp. Under the stars. What do you think?"

"Sure." She yawned and rubbed her eyes. "That would be nice."

Even though the genesis of the idea to go camping sprung from her father's demise, Collin thoroughly enjoyed preparing for the trip. By Wednesday, his truck was packed and organized before she came home from class.

She bypassed the garage and went to flop down on the couch. "I can't wait to get out of this fucking heat. I'm sweating like a pig."

"Once you cool off, come out to the garage. I need you to help me with the last bit of packing."

"Collin, we're only going away for three or four days, it's not like we are going off the grid for a month." She referenced the endless supplies neatly squared away in his truck. "Are we ever coming home?"

She was stripped down to a tank, shorts, and flip flops when she ventured into his garage. Her hair was tied up in a messy bun on top of her head. She paused in the doorway, as if waiting for an invitation to enter his area.

"Come here." The ever-present cigarette caused a thin line of smoke to rise from the old, upside-down piston that served as an ashtray on his work bench. "I want you to pack our emergency kit."

An array of survival and first aid supplies were scattered around a rusted metal tool box that was roughly the size of a briefcase. It had been completely black at some point. The last time Collin was at his parents' house (before it became his mom's house), he snagged it from the garage, figuring it would come in handy at some point. He finished wiping the dust off it and a screech from its rusty hinges greeted her when he opened it up like a clam shell. He produced a list of items. She read it out loud:

- o   Strike anywhere matches in a waterproof case
- o   Flint and Steel
- o   Water purification tablets
- o   Signal mirror
- o   Emergency blanket
- o   Small first aid kit
- o   Knife
- o   Compass
- o   550 cord

"You need me to pack this?" she asked.

"I want you to pack it."

She shrugged and didn't ask why. Instead, she matched up the items on the table to the list and organized it all neatly in the box. He asked her to double-check, and so she did, awaiting his approval.

He closed the box without looking inside. "I trust you," he said as he handed it to her. "Will you put it in the truck?"

"Anywhere?"

"Put it where you'll be able to get it right away if you need to."

After securing the tool box behind the passenger seat, she brushed her hands together. "Anything else? CPR training? Bear whistle? Just in case?" she mocked.

"Go get dressed in your gear for camping. We'll leave at sixteen hundred."

Her face scrunched up.

Collin sighed in exasperation. "That's four o'clock, Lauren, jeez...."

The first two days up in the pines of Mt. Charleston was an unexpected decompression session for them both. He didn't realize how oppressive the heat really was down in the city. At 10,000 feet, the air was cool—crisp even— and he could finally breathe. Not to mention his craving for nicotine had waned. Lauren's face melted into ease, replacing the furrowed brow that threatened to crack at any moment over the past week.

He was surprised at how much she enjoyed the simplicity of being isolated in nature. He hadn't pegged her for much of an outdoorsy type of girl, but it suited her. Something about the connection to him, in nature, opened her up and she talked about her childhood.

There were stories of her great-aunt, Pamela, who had raised her with a healthy dose of Native American mythology. Specifically, Inuit mythology. They were the indigenous people inhabiting the most northern parts of Canada and Alaska. They were more like Eskimos than Indians and reclaimed their lands, causing the Northwest Territories to become Nunavut. Collin knew a little about Pamela from before this excursion, but it wasn't until a hike that he put two and two together—Lauren was part Native American. A small part, her mother was born to a man who was either Dutch or German (Lauren wasn't sure which), and her Grandmother was only half-Inuit.

With Lauren under the care of Pamela, her mother's attentions turned to her own social life, constantly searching for "Mr. Right." When Collin broached the topic of Lauren's dad, he'd get, "He left before I turned two, what more is there to say?" in response.

By the third night, they were efficient at setting up for the night. It was a good thing, since there was no moon in the sky. Lauren crawled out of the tent, where she had been smoothing out their sleeping bags, and slipped on her shoes before zipping it back up.

"You should put another log on the fire, it's dying," she observed.

"Will you go get that emergency kit from the truck?" he asked, not making any move toward the wood stack.

"Are you okay?"

"Yeah, just go get it."

She returned a moment later with it and started over to her chair next to the fire. "Seriously, Collin, the fire's almost out."

"I know, come take a walk with me. Bring the box."

She took his hand and followed him away from their campsite. He had set up a mat with a couple rolled-up sleeping bags that could serve as pillows in a nearby clearing. By the time they'd settled down on it, they couldn't see anything—the fire, the campsite, his truck—it was eerie. And with zero moonlight, they could barely see each other.

"Look at those stars," she whispered. "My God."

"Do you remember when we first met? I told you how the only thing from the Gulf I'd want you to experience was the night sky?"

"Yes."

"This is as close as it gets. It's something, isn't it?"

She started to recline, her head aimed for the rolled-up sleeping bag, but he stopped her. She sat up cross-legged, facing him.

He placed the tool box between them and the same squeal broke the silence when he opened it. "I want you to pull out the knife from inside without disturbing anything else in there."

"I can't see anything. Do you have a flashlight?"

"No. Think about where you placed it when you packed it. And use your fingertips to feel around the inside, identifying the other contents will help. Your mind should be able to visualize what you're touching, and you need to think logically. 'What did I put it next to? Was it wrapped in plastic? If it shifted, would it still be next to that item? What does it feel like?' Ask yourself those questions." A miniscule screech occurred when he switched to his right hand to hold open the lid. "I need to oil that," he muttered. "This is how we had to exist at night. We were on one hundred percent light discipline in the Gulf. By the time the sun went down, you had to know where everything was, especially your bed."

"Hmm, okay." She pulled her hand back immediately after her fingertips brushed the rim.

"The knife," he reminded her.

"Right." She started to reach in again, but once more, abruptly pulled her hand back. Into her chest this time.

"What's wrong?"

She chuckled nervously. "Um, I don't know, I just...." She sat up straighter and cleared her throat. "Okay, the knife, got it." This time her hand slid slowly to the open box. She was holding her breath.

Stiff from sitting so still, Collin tilted his head from one side to the other.

She recoiled.

He dropped the lid and it shut with a smack. "What is it?" When he placed his hand on her shoulder, she damn near jumped out of her skin. "Lauren?"

Her voice was husky and trembled when she answered. "I keep thinking you're going to snap the lid down on my fingers. It's so stupid, I know." She forced a laugh that came out as a sort of cough. "Let's try again."

He didn't open it back up, but chose his words carefully once he surmised the real reason behind her reaction. Talking about her dad wasn't going to help her move through her mistrust of men. He needed to prove to her that she could trust him. "Listen, honey, you need to know that I would never do something like that. I wouldn't get any pleasure scaring you or even startling you. I want you to trust me. I can't force you to. You need to come to that on your own." He itched for a smoke. "Think about it this way, I trusted you enough to pack up the essential things we'd need to survive if, God forbid, something happened to us up here. Also, I want you to rely on yourself. I know you can do this, to use your sense of touch and logic to get that knife in complete darkness. I would never, never, let that lid fall down on your fingers." The stiffness in her body had fallen away. "Do you want to try again?"

She nodded.

This exercise went on for the next twenty minutes. By the end of it, she could take everything out in order and pack it up again in the same manner. All while he held the lid open. Their conversation turned to what he thought about when lying under the stars in the Gulf. Then he eased her down to recline next to him.

"Most times, I only thought about this." He pulled her to face him and kissed her, gently. His tongue touched her lips, looking for permission to enter.

She granted it and scooted in closer. Since they began dating, he spent a great deal of time evaluating her body. It was a mix of curved muscles and soft flesh that created instant arousal at the very thought of it.

And that night, under 100% light restriction, he relied on his sense of touch to experience it.

A few weeks later, her grades came in the mail, and he opened them before she came home. All As, except for one B-. He took her out to dinner to celebrate, noting the marked difference in how she carried herself in public.

All she needed was for someone to believe in her, he thought while watching her gracefully sip red wine. *Elegance* was the word that came to his mind.

"What?" she inquired with a smile.

"I'm really impressed with you." It was the truth.

"Thank you." She opened her mouth to say something, but hesitated.

"Tell me what's on your mind," he encouraged in a soft voice.

"I'm in love with you." Expectation oozed out of her eyes as she held her breath.

"Well, now I'm even more in awe of you. You took the thoughts right out of my head."

The waiter set down her plate, breaking the moment. She shrunk back as he did the parmesan and refilled her water. Collin thanked him and said they were fine for now.

He took her hand before she picked up a fork. "I love you, too."

Nothing further had to be said, he knew that she was secure and confident. There was no need to gush on and on to convince her that he truly did love her. Later that night, he made love to her without imagining she was Stephanie at any point in bed...or after. It was a first,

and not being burdened with the guilt he had always experienced afterward was immensely satisfying.

c h a p t e r   t w e l v e

The Hard Rock Hotel and Casino

"Tyler will be here tomorrow!" Lauren broke into a cute, little "happy dance" in front of the TV. The ragged hem of Collin's old Combat Engineer Unit T-shirt—the one she claimed immediately after moving in—caught some air and exposed her boy shorts. The T-shirt looked like it was being fluttered out before being hung to dry as she shimmied over to Collin. When she dropped the portable phone on the couch, half of it disappeared between the cushions.

It was August 31, 2001. The last day of summer school and the first day of a Labor Day weekend, or "epic" as Lauren dubbed it, once she found out that Tyler was coming to town. He had booked a suite at the Hard Rock that included the most sought after VIP cabana by the pool. Lauren suppressed her relief that

Thom wasn't coming…with Tyler, anyway. Collin was the audience to an enthusiastic spiel though.

"Commercial's over, sit down." Collin pulled her back to the couch after a playful smack on her rear.

The giggling subsided and her face nestled into his shoulder with a muffled squeal of excitement before she calmed down to watch the end of *The Daily Show with Jon Stewart*. She loved the comfort between them. Ever since their camping trip, the blossoming of self-reliance in all areas of her life fostered a more authentic persona. No longer did she worry about saying something stupid or immature in front of him. When they discussed things, she expressed her thoughts and emotions with truth, no longer censoring herself.

"Here it is, ladies and gentlemen, your moment of Zen," Jon Stewart concluded the show. A movie clip from a corny sci-fi movie came on the screen. A very buff, shirtless, British actor had a green alien pressed against a wall. The camera focused in first on his glistening muscles from the rear and then it cut to the wanton expression on the alien's face. Her mouth parted as she succumbed to him.

"Helena, Queen of the Tigerians, trust me to have a great care for your heart." His smooth accent carried an unspoken promise of the most heart-stopping, sexual communion in all the galaxy, no doubt.

Helena's head reared up to meet his gaze. "Ours is a heartless race."

Both Collin and Lauren were engrossed in this campy scene. Lauren's hand twitched when the camera focused in on the actor's torso once more.

"Then I will have a great care for your ass." He kissed her with so much passion that it seemed like he wasn't acting.

Collin's head tilted back with an "Oh, my God!" and Lauren's dropped into her palm, shaking, as she groaned, "Oh nooooo!"

Still chuckling, Collin stood and returned their ice cream bowls to the kitchen.

After a quick glance over her shoulder, she snatched up the TiVo remote and pressed rewind. She wasn't quick enough to hit stop before Collin appeared in the doorway. Lauren had leaned forward on the couch, completely unaware of his presence.

His laugh startled her just as the end of the movie scene replayed on the TV. She dropped the remote, and with a crack, all the batteries spilled out. She bumped her shin when she shot over to the TV to manually turn off the power. She was an ungainly sight after getting caught checking out that shirtless James Bayer guy again...even blushing.

Collin's eyes were easy with amusement. "Looks like I need to get Showtime for you now. Why don't you come over here and let *me* have a care for *your* ass."

The sound of her own giggle surprised her. It'd been months since she heard it and now here it was again, twice already. But, it was the perfect night to be sexy and silly. She peeled off the T-shirt and flung it back to the couch before she reached him.

He pressed her up to the wall and kissed her passionately, setting the tone for the rest of the holiday weekend.

"Day Dream" on Namasea was based on a notorious daytime pool party that took place every Sunday at the Hard Rock Hotel and Casino. Recreating it on the ship required hours of research to be done by way of watching the first season of *Re-Hab: Party at the Hard Rock Hotel,* and uncut, archived episodes of MTV's *The Grind.* It had been filmed there regularly during the late 1990s. Creating the atmosphere solely on memory would have been...uh...tricky.

Even though he'd moved to L.A. after graduation, Tyler reigned over the scene at the HRC for that entire weekend and a sizable entourage of the most attractive men had materialized. But, Lauren was able to get him alone for a couple hours on Sunday, when she and Collin met him for lunch at the Forum Shops.

"Thom is scouting out new studio locations." Tyler spoke loudly over the echoing noise from the crashing water. They were having espressos at Bertolini's, seated at a table so close to the gigantic fountain that Lauren's hair was frizzy by the end of lunch.

Collin picked up the bill before the words, "Whenever you're ready," finished coming out of the server's mouth.

Tyler protested, but Collin insisted. After an appreciative look toward Collin, Tyler suggested they shop around for a bit. "Let's get some new gear for tomorrow." Collin was a good sport about it all, letting Tyler pick out (and pay for) some stylish trunks and sunglasses.

"Do you guys want to come over tonight? You can just spend the night on the pullout," Tyler offered to Lauren while they browsed through some outrageously expensive men's T-shirts. Collin had gone out for a smoke, leaving them with the only few moments they've had completely alone together in months.

"No, you have fun with your group tonight. We'll come by first thing tomorrow."

Tyler stopped flipping through the rack and faced her. "You seem content. Is everything going as well as I imagine it to be?"

She didn't contain the obvious beam of happiness that appeared whenever anyone asked about Collin. They were exclusive and she loved to go on and on about him. "He's so calm about everything and never patronizes me. I...." She clasped Tyler's wrist. "I told him I loved him and he said it back." Her grasp released and she stepped back, awaiting his reaction.

Tyler's expression was one of an older brother, tempering the excitement about her crush until the lecture began. "That's great, hon, just remember, you still have your whole life ahead of you. Don't get me wrong...I like Collin and he's been good for you. Really good. There's no need for you to jump into any rash decisions, okay? That's all I'm saying, just take things slowly...one day at a time." Pride overtook his reprimanding attitude. "Look at you, you're two semesters away from a degree. Who'd have thought?"

Lauren bit her tongue. Instant defensiveness about the love of her life threatened to erupt into an emotionally charged justification. After all, the next day was his final blowout party and she was itching for some excitement. Getting into a disagreement with Tyler would ruin it.

He means well.... She conceded and nodded in agreement.

When Collin and Lauren arrived at the hub of decadence the following day, bottle service had already been set up and the who's who of the gay scene in Vegas populated the tent. Lauren fell right back into her party-girl sidekick role. Stripped down to a crocheted bikini that left nothing to the imagination, she served as a deterrent for any girls who meandered their way.

Loose from a couple drinks and inspired by the Middle Eastern techno music, Lauren smoothly knelt in front of Collin to slip a tab of ecstasy in his mouth. She rose, and in complete harem-girl fashion, tipped the glass of champagne from her other hand to his lips. A bead of sweat rolled down her belly.

Then, right in time with the music, she rolled her hips like a belly dancer and slinked away to set down the champagne flute. With both hands free, her entire body glided right past the whole of Tyler's inner circle. They were all squished up around Collin—he was sitting smack in the middle of the daybed—watching her enticing show.

A large water pitcher balanced atop her head as she danced. The gays were captivated as if entranced by her audacity. She hoped that Collin found it to be a sensual show, dedicated to him. There wasn't another straight man in sight.

With a commanding pause, she faced the group and her right arm floated up in a port-a-bras to clasp the handle. Her ability to simply bring the pitcher down in front of her in the way one strokes a lover caused the group to collectively lurch toward her.

Fast as a rabbit, she went to fling the water at everyone on the daybed. She was just faking them out, though; she was swift to pull the pitcher back into her. A wave rolled up over the rim and soaked her chest. Tyler, who had been standing behind the group, fell out laughing when all those queens, including Collin, jumped up, screaming like women. Lauren had to set down the pitcher to wipe her eyes, she was laughing so hard. She'd almost forgotten how much fun it was on days like this.

As people came in and out of their VIP area, Collin and Lauren came in and out of focus. She let her eyes close halfway so that the flashes of fuchsia, neon green, and white blurred together. Urine, glitter, and sweat mingled in the aqua water, but no one seemed to care as the wall of bodies squeezed into the wading pools serving as a holding tank for the daytime club.

Lauren was peaking from the X when she let the base of her pussy rest against Collin's stiff erection, once settled on his lap in the pool. That same giggle bubbled up when he primitively muttered that he wouldn't be able to stand up anytime soon. Her back pressed against his chest. She pulled his hand around her waist and slid it down the front of her bikini bottom. Her breath sucked in as his fingers relaxed, as if ready to spread her cleft. But before she could exhale, they clenched back, and he yanked his hand out of her bottoms.

"Later," was his garbled response as he squeezed her breast…so hard she visibly winced. With that, he gave her a small, but definite, shove off his lap, causing her to splash a couple of guys next to them.

One shot her a scathing look, but the other touched his shoulder and shook his head. The irritated one faced Collin head-on with a blatant erection pointing directly at him. Lauren's head whipped back to Collin, in hopes that by some small miracle he didn't notice that guy's display. Collin hastily stood and stepped out of the pool.

His admirer wailed, "Whatever, soldier boy!" with a flirty splash of the water that mostly drenched Lauren.

"Stop it!" she snapped back at them before going after Collin. When she stepped out of the pool, her vision momentarily blackened and she swayed. It passed and she treaded lightly on the cement path to catch up to him without hurting her feet. When she found him, he was leaning into their cocktail waitress on the side of the cabana. His mouth was at her ear, saying something that caused her to bite her lower lip. His hand dropped to her waist and he pulled her close into his chest with a possessive grasp on the hollow of her hipbone.

Lauren froze. Even though X dulled the jealous side of her personality, this scene stirred a flash of white anger. It took great effort for her to make a casual approach.

"Hi," she said with forced gaiety and she squeezed between them. It was awkward. "Bring another bottle over for the ice bucket," she directed to the waitress.

The waitress retreated, but continued to hold eye contact with Collin as if Lauren was invisible.

"Please, sweetheart," Lauren purred with bitterness. She turned her back on the waitress and looped her arms around Collin's neck. A press of the breast against his pecks and the tip of her tongue on his lips would hopefully send any thoughts of that waitress straight out the door.

Since she was almost positive that Collin had never taken X before, Lauren decided to let go of his coziness with yet another bimbo she'd seen him with earlier.

A few hours later, Tyler and his friends settled the check and were off to the after party, leaving the cabana empty for Lauren and Collin. The crowd had thinned considerably and the vibe of the pool party mellowed. The check was settled. To ensure no further chance for meddling cocktail waitresses to drop by, Lauren untied the cabana's ropes, allowing the privacy flaps to fall. This base camp that had been a free-for-all since 11:00 a.m. transformed into an enclosed 9x9 space occupied by one couple. An echo of warmth remained in the dry, desert air as the sun descended in the west.

Lauren lost herself for a moment. She was caught up in the gorgeous sunset while standing naked in the private shower off the back. Chlorine swirled down the drain as she pressed her hands against her freezing white breasts. She snapped out of it when the water gurgled in the pipe. She wrung out her hair and secured it up in a top knot. Her sheer cover-up unevenly stuck to the tops of her thighs.

The scene, the music, and the drugs emboldened her. She was recharged from being among her tribe, and one of the gays left her with two more tabs of X. Collin washed one down before she stepped into the shower. She popped the last one and slid into the scarlet den to find him relaxing on that same teak daybed. Under the canopy, his smoke rings floated toward the shadows of people going by outside.

A different kind of tent had poked up from his crotch and the laces on his board shorts had been loosened. When Lauren sank down in front of him, his hand trembled as he stubbed out a cigarette. An effect from the drug, most likely.

Without a word, he rose and hoisted her up by the shoulders like she was a rag doll. White half-moons appeared at the base of his fingernails as his mouth crushed hers. Overcome by his aggressive grab and the potent smell of tobacco mixed with beer, Lauren's desire mounted. She didn't hold back her roving tongue that explored his mouth. Her stance didn't waver and she began to tug at his shorts.

He pulled away with an irritated grunt and kept her at arm's length, forcing her writhing body to a standstill.

Lauren's mind ran in a million different directions. *Is he pissed off? Is this an act setting up an evening of primal fucking? Is he confused? Does he want to make love? Maybe I'm coming on too strong....* The accumulation of his actions that day had cut her down to size and humiliation took up residence in her psyche. The next natural move would have been for him to go in for more of her mouth, her breasts, her everything, but he didn't.

His eyes squeezed shut. "It's just us now."

She desperately wished he'd look at her. "What? What do you mean?" Her voice shook as she stammered out, "I'm sorry, what did I do? Collin? Is...I mean...don't you want it to be just us?"

At last his eyes opened, gigantic pupils overwhelmed her as he seemed to strain himself from snapping at her. "I've wanted it to be just us from the moment you landed in front of me. I need to know if there's anyone else." The last few words rang with accusation.

She was on shaky ground, confused, but then the words poured out and confidence reigned. "Listen to me, listen to my voice. Listen to my intention, Collin.

You have *owned* every sensual thought I've ever had in my *life*. I may not have known it until you found me, but once you did, there was no turning back. Any orgasm I've ever had, *ever*, anytime my mouth has *ever* salivated with desire, it's only because of you. Don't you understand? I'm just an observer to my own desires, but you, you're the one who controls them."

His grip relaxed and one hand traveled down to capture her sex.

She held off the urge to grind into his fingers, still needing him to say something that would make her feel safe with him.

The gentle rubbing on her labia turned to desperate pawing. "God, I want you," he confessed in a defeated way that sounded like him again.

Lauren exhaled with satisfaction and her body synced up to his touch. It was just the X, she felt certain of that. And the timing was right; he should be starting to peak from the second one he took.

"I love you," rolled off her tongue.

Both hands now, groping her every crevice, he'd finally surrendered to doing what they were supposed to be doing in this scenario.

"Say that again," he groaned in desperation as his mouth found her neck.

"I love your dick." Her legs were giving out.

"Yeah, you do."

Lauren blinked, unsure if he was being condescending or not.

Collin did the only thing left to do; he spread her out on the daybed, and fucked her harder than he ever had before.

After they both came, Lauren realized that a throw pillow had managed to wedge up under her neck. She grabbed it and chucked it across the tent. The unexpected motion broke the heaviness in the atmosphere and they cracked up laughing.

Relief washed over her.

Never again, she thought, *we are never doing this again.*

chapter thirteen

Collin's Place
LATER THAT NIGHT

Collin folded up his itinerary and dropped it on the nightstand before collapsing into bed. He silently cursed at himself for printing it out just moments after coming home. The week leading up to Labor Day, she unsuccessfully attempted to hide her disappointment about his upcoming trip to New York. He assumed a visit with Tyler would pacify her yearning to come with him. Now, after today…the cabana…that whole…he didn't know how to classify the past twelve hours. Or how it would affect their relationship moving forward.

Why did he feel the need to do that?! The reason eluded him—sort of. He knew damn well it would bother her. Perhaps it was a lingering bad influence that decided to stay, even after peaking on X.

Certain she would climb in bed any moment, he turned to his side, and squeezed his eyes shut. He prayed that he'd regain control of his mind, perhaps once the drug was completely out of his system. The familiar noise of her brushing her teeth faded away as his compromised thoughts rewound back in time.

When Collin was a child, he'd often wake up in the middle of the night to a red figure looming over him. The first few times it happened, he screamed, causing his concerned parents to stumble in half-asleep. The figure would dissipate into smoke the instant the door opened, leaving him to wail in his mother's arms. She'd brush off his incoherent claims of a "Red One" who invaded his room at night. Silently, his father would just stare out the window, listening as his mother would begin to eventually scold Collin for waking them up in the middle of the night.

"Stop filling his head with your stupid curse!" he heard her hiss at his dad in the hall.

Around age ten or eleven, Dad took him shooting for the first time, which doubled as an official initiation into the St. Germain family curse. After several tries to hit a target a mere twenty-five yards away, Dad told him to take a break. Collin couldn't remember the specifics of that conversation, but it didn't matter, he was continuously reminded of the details for years to come.

Something happened to his dad's father during WWII. He saw something, a red leader from the djinn race bearing the name Iblis. The first-time Collin's grandfather saw IT, he was hiding behind a curtain as IT provided intel to a group of Nazi soldiers. Collin's grandfather was a POW, being held by those same Nazis.

"Your grandfather helped changed the course of World War Two. But…at a price."

Collin never got the full story until he came back from the Gulf War. All he needed to know prior to that was the part about how all St. Germain men were cursed to marry beautiful, but adulterous, women.

Iblis continued to appear in Collin's room at night, but eventually he stopped crying for his parents. Even though he couldn't always see Iblis, the nearly inaudible mutterings from IT continually seeped into Collin's thoughts. Those mutterings became twisted temptations that Collin desperately wanted to act upon during his adolescence. Temptations driven by fantasies that most teenage boys think about, but never actually act upon. The more devious the act, the more Iblis enticed him with the ability to do it.

The discipline over both mind and body that the Corps provided is what finally exorcised Iblis from Collin's psyche. As a young Marine, he excelled, developed a tough exterior, and created a mental defense mechanism that eventually blocked Iblis from gaining access to his mind. LCpl St. Germain became an expert at resisting any impulse to experiment in the dark end of his imagination. Iblis became a faded memory and IT's constant offers to grant Collin wishes ceased by the time he made Cpl.

Except once....

The image of rolling through the desert to clear minefields on the way to Kuwait City dropped into his mind as the bed sank from Lauren getting under the covers. She must have gotten his message, because she instantly turned her back on him as well.

He regretted going along with her idea to take X together. It had to have been the drug that stripped away his barriers and knocked on a door that had been locked for years. Once opened, it must have initiated a transmission that traveled into the ethers and invited Iblis to come out.

And play.

The effects of the pill had come on strong and fast almost immediately after Lauren fed him the first one. Then his perception of her became skewed. It was disgusting, her suggestive dancing and the way she tried to get him to practically finger fuck her in the pool. Downright whorish—that was a more accurate description. He tried pushing her away a few times during the day, but she refused to leave him alone.

He sought refuge parked at the bar while she was caught up in nonsense conversations with Tyler's friends—faggots—several meters away. He couldn't help but scrutinize her from his vantage point. His internal dissertation came to a crescendo and he scraped the bottom of his barstool in a rush to go tell her how fucking stupid she was acting. An image of what her reaction would be as he degraded her in front of everyone was tempting. Afterwards, he'd force her head....

The guy next to him tapped his shoulder. "Gotta light?"

"Yeah...here." Collin tossed the lighter and spied the fresh bucket of beer in front of him. A beer, that's what he needed to get his brain in order. A cold beer.

Before he asked, the guy offered him one. "Go ahead, get it out now so it doesn't get mixed in with the rest."

A few gulps did the trick. Collin regained his bearings and looked to the distraction of these two guys. They just might keep the dark side at bay. He didn't mean to judge her like that, he loved her. He grasped to remember this was all a trick, brought on by the drug, this wasn't reality.

A few bullshit exchanges between him and the guys with the beer went by. He couldn't exactly recall what was said; it was all most likely centering on the crude descriptions they came up with to classify every girl who walked by. Within moments, Collin was trapped once more in the red haze that had found its way back into his mind. Perhaps from the brutishness of their conversation.

Collin was cut off mid-sentence when the guy on the other side dropped something. The talker punched his arm as he scrambled to pick it up. It was a small, plastic bottle...like eye drops. They were fucking idiots, shuffling to pick up a bottle of Visine off the floor. Collin smirked at his assessment, not caring if they noticed or not.

The last thing he recalled thinking, before everything went red, was something to do with saline solution.

What happens if you drink Visine? Had he ever put it in one of his buddies' beers? Maybe it was one of those things that gives someone the runs. They were always doing stupid shit like that in the barracks.

One of the guys pointed to Lauren. The two honed in on her, leaning right over Collin to get a better look.

Collin must have said something that indicated he knew her.

"Those tits," the closer guy began. "You've had some of that? Jesus, is she as tasty as she looks? I'd claim both holes, maybe start with her pussy but finish off in the back door." He squeezed a few extra drops into one of the beer bottles.

Collin attempted in vain to focus in on the red lettering on the dropper. Focusing on something would help, but there was no label on it. It was just a travel-sized bottle, like from Target, for shampoo.

"You mind?" the guy asked Collin, already on his feet with a dosed beer in hand.

Collin didn't need to squint to make out Iblis smiling over the exchange with his blessing.

"Go ahead," Collin mumbled with a shrug.

The guy hustled, but Collin had an unexpected change of heart and caught his arm.

He yanked it away in irritation. "What?"

"Dude, I was kidding. She's my fucking girlfriend." It was a weak thing to say after giving this asshole the go-ahead to…to…. Collin's head cleared, not wanting to think about what would happen next if she drank that beer.

Perhaps the guy sensed that he was a loose cannon. Or it could have been something about Collin's ever-present military air that made him brush off the interaction with a "whatever" and leave. His friend hoisted up the bucket of beer and followed suit.

Collin clapped both palms on his cheeks several times in a row in an attempt to clear his head.

Jesus, what the fuck just happened?

Lauren called his name from the other side of the bar area. As he made his way to her, she blew him a kiss. An errant memory of Stephanie flowed through his thoughts. It was something about Lauren's crocheted bikini; Steph would have loved it. Of course, she wouldn't do it justice the way Lauren did, but she'd try. Picturing Steph when he looked at Lauren, it dampened the despicable things running through his head, so he kept up the charade. For the rest of the day, it wasn't Lauren's face he saw, it was Stephanie's. It was the only thing that might get him through the rest of the day.

He hadn't wished that Lauren was Stephanie during sex ever since she moved in. Before that, he regularly conjured up Stephanie's face as he rocked over Lauren in passion. Her memory fulfilled him in a way that was unparalleled compared to his sweet Lauren.

As the drug started to wear off, Stephanie disappeared. Sometimes, light from a passing car streamed in as he turned down Harmon and illuminated Lauren's dark hair, making it appear blonde for a split second. He indulged in imagining Lauren as a blonde, like *her,* for an instant. He was quick to chastise himself and by the time they made it home, he could look over at Lauren without seeing Steph's features.

No more.

Stephanie had done a number on him. To think that even with a gorgeous, twenty-one-year-old who followed him around like a puppy…that he *still* fell into the "what-ifs" was emasculating. He should have been able to forget that cheating bitch forever ago.

Maybe Steph was his curse.

Back in bed, Lauren's breathing evened out as he rationalized that it was just because he was going to New York on Friday for a Marine Corps reunion with his buddies from the Gulf—that's all. Gearing up to reminisce about those times brought Stephanie front and center in his mind. The drugs had made it worse and he vowed to never take X again.

At last, sleep came and brought relief.

Collin was still foggy when he woke up the next day. He'd forgotten the previous day's events upon rousing. For that cherished, but brief lapse, he relished in the view of Lauren's figure sitting on the edge of the bed. Love was the only word worthy enough to describe the emotion stirring inside him. He was inundated with a strong desire to protect her. The instinct painfully reminded him of the lack of protection he offered yesterday. "What time is it?" he asked.

"Noon."

"Are you going somewhere?"

"Yoga.

Her voice was soft and carried no emotion. Maybe everything was okay.

"I'm going to sleep for a while longer. Wake me when you get home?"

She nodded, but made no move to get up. An air of expectation came over her posture.

"I'm going to miss you while I'm gone," he tried. "I'll be thinking of you the whole time."

It was just the prompt that led her to mildly plead her case. "I...I was just thinking, maybe I could use some airline miles and go too. I won't get in your way. I don't need to go out with you guys or anything and I won't ask you where you've been or tell you what time to come back. I'd just love to see New York and I'll keep myself occupied."

He sincerely wanted to say yes to her at that moment. He couldn't though—no girlfriends—rule number one of the weekend. He sat up straighter. "Babe, I can't. I know you're disappointed. I'm sorry. I'll take you back there in the spring and we'll stay in the city, at a nice hotel. We're going to be in Brooklyn, a shithole. You don't want to go there and no one's bringing their wives or girlfriends, it's not that kind of thing."

He could tell by the way she sucked in her breath that she was debating whether to push the topic. All he wanted to do was go back to sleep. Fortunately, she just dropped a kiss on his forehead and left for the day.

Collin nestled back under the covers and fell into a dreamy state until the phone rang a half an hour later.

Usually, he would have just let the machine get it, but an outside force nudged him to answer. Sunlight filtered through the gauzy burgundy curtains, casting a hazy glow over the bedroom.

If only Lauren had stayed home, he thought. He was ready for another round.

Stephanie's voice reached his ear once he picked up the phone. "Collin?"

She had him by the balls when he answered, literally. There was just enough X in his system that kept his hand steadily pumping his erection ever since Lauren left, keeping the edge of orgasm at bay.

The stroking welcomed the sound of his ex's voice. "...Donna and I have become really close. Marshall's sister, she came to Vegas with him, do you remember her? She told me you'd all be in the city this weekend for the reunion." Steph's words were irrelevant; it was just having her with him, purring into his ear mere seconds before his explosion that mattered. His wish had been granted.

But she was rambling and the names ran together.

Marshall? She means Mayhem.

The date, the year, the place, it was all so vague. The current time and location slipped away from him as the euphoric wave threatened to crash. Just a few more pulls, hard ones that stretched the skin, and it would be all over. Stephanie had to have known what his stifled moans meant. She spelled out his favorite fantasy, the same one from when it was his turn in the phone booth behind the barracks. Every Tuesday at 9:00 p.m.

"Donna said you looked so hot when she was there visiting, but I need to see for myself. Not just see, but...." Damn, the exquisite articulation of what she would do, in person, to bring him to climax hadn't faltered over the years.

"Even if you are still dating that child," rolled off her tongue at the height of his orgasm.

Semen oozing across his stomach and sticking to the sheet made him feel dirty, but it waned next to the self-loathing he felt when Stephanie voiced her concern for Lauren. Guilt: that was her other forte. Apparently, Donna had plenty to say about the age difference between Collin and Lauren.

Cut from the same cloth, those two....

"Have you considered that you could be exploiting her?" she asked, like a therapist might to a cheating husband during a counseling session. "She's younger than both your sisters. Imagine how you'd feel if some guy, a decade older no less, had one of them in his bed." Her voice rose. "The Collin I knew would have killed the ped...fucker."

His youngest sister's face, all round and innocent, flashed in his mind and it made him cringe.

"It looks bad," Stephanie advised, now with her "preacher's wife" voice. "Not just to me, but to Marshall. In fact, he was the one most concerned about it when they got back from Vegas."

There was still some time before boarding began for the 2:30 p.m. flight leaving McCarren for LaGuardia on Friday, September 7, 2001. Too much time. The past few days had been trying between Collin and Lauren. This break, it couldn't have come at a better time. For Collin, at least, the mind-fuck that began Monday carried repercussions that he kept hidden from Lauren. "You don't have to wait here if you don't want to," he said with formality to her profile. Her magazine had been opened to the same Lancôme ad since they sat down at the gate.

"It's fine." She flipped the page.

Collin's cell phone rang. Mayhem, finally!

Just Marshall these days.

Collin had plenty of time to analyze what Steph said after their unexpected phone sex. By Thursday, the guilt turned to resentment, and he called Mayhem to hash it out. But, the machine picked up and Mayhem managed to call him back at precisely the wrong fucking time. Certain that Lauren wasn't going to budge from her seat, Collin strolled over to the post card rack.

She hastily crossed her legs and sat up straighter. She was trying to appear indifferent and failing miserably at it.

"Where's she living again?" Collin repeated, in a clear voice, once he was out of earshot.

"Just over the bridge, about two hours I'd say. Maybe three. She's got the two kids and things have been rocky between her and Dan."

"I told her I'd come." Collin thumbed through the postcards, briefly forgetting the real reason he wanted to talk to Mayhem.

"Yeah, I know, I heard all about it. Seriously, what the fuck were you thinking, bro?"

Collin smacked the display, nearly causing it to fall. "She said you were worried I was some kind of pedophile out here that needed to be put in check, bro!"

Mayhem laughed. "Do you really fucking believe anything those two would cook up? Jesus, Collin, where's your head? Lauren's fine," he drew out the long "I" in fine. "Sweet, pretty...obviously devoted to you. They're just jealous, that's all."

"Where'd she come up with Lauren being ten years younger, a 'decade' she'd said. She's only eight years...." Ugh, it sounded creepy. "I know, I know, but she's twenty-one. Hardly a kid."

"Grover, you've been off the rez for a while, haven't you? I wouldn't give a shit if she was sixteen. Why do you care so much?"

It was so silent that Collin thought the call had been dropped.

"Grover?"

He couldn't even tell his best friend the truth; that he was obsessed with Stephanie. Even after everything she did while they were in the Gulf. He cleared his throat. "The boy, Charles? He's gotta be nine, ten…?"

Mayhem cut him off and repeated the same thing he always did about her older son. "She'll always have a warm spot for you. But she's not giving anything up about Charles unless you go back to her and stay. She's not leaving Jersey, so if you're that desperate for a rerun with two kids, *stepkids*, then come home and stay, if that's what you want. But, there ain't nothing wrong with Vegas, especially when you're enjoying life with a sweet little girlfriend."

Collin didn't answer. It bothered him to have Mayhem discuss Lauren, like she was the obvious choice. And he was determined to see Steph while he was back east. He had to touch her and see if she still brought out that insatiable lust.

No need to explain it to Mayhem, though. Collin ended their conversation with a non-committal, "Well, we'll just have to see," and then he brought a Diet Coke over to Lauren as a peace offering.

She smiled and placed a soft, lingering kiss on his lips in thanks. Instead of speaking up, she took a sip.

"Little Miss Lauri can't hold a grudge for longer than a phone conversation. Do you really think someone who's that weak will ever be able to remain faithful?" Iblis whispered in Collin's ear.

Right before he could ask Lauren if she heard that, his boarding group was announced over the loud speaker.

"It's too bad I don't have a cell. I don't want to miss any calls from you," she said wistfully.

"When I get back, we'll go get you one, okay?" He leaned over for one last kiss, and for that moment, all the chatter taking up residence in his head diminished. He was too enrapt by a mouth that continuously received his with eagerness.

chapter fourteen

West Coast
9/11

Since Collin wasn't coming home until Wednesday, Lauren decided she would walk up to her favorite coffee shop, Café Copioh, and do nothing but hang out on that sunny Tuesday morning. That cute barista still worked there and he liked to flirt with her. Not that she would do anything, but some attention would be nice. She took a shower listening to a yoga mantra CD while humming to herself. With no job, no classes, no Collin, and no Tyler, there was no real agenda for the day.

Something seemed off during her walk up Harmon toward UNLV. The street was empty and quieter than usual. She arrived at a strip mall across the street from campus thirty minutes later. Through the window outside the coffee shop, she saw a cluster of people crowded around the counter. A couple of girls were crying at a table next to the door when Lauren stepped in and surveyed the scene. No one was making coffee, no one was ordering. A hanging bell choked a jangle when the door closed behind her, marking the moment her perspective shifted and the floor dropped out from underneath her.

The TV mounted behind the counter was on with the volume turned all the way up.

Lauren pushed her way to the counter and saw the barista, CUPPAJOE. She waved him over.

He was annoyed at first, possibly thinking she might want to order. But once his eyes peeled away from the screen, he hurried over to her. "Can you fucking believe this?" he asked her.

Lauren was white as a sheet and felt like she might pass out. "Your phone," she gasped. "Can I use your phone, my boyfriend, oh, my God...." she trailed off. Was Collin in Manhattan or Brooklyn? She didn't remember. She didn't even really know the difference between them or where the Twin Towers were in relation to him. All she knew was that Collin was in New York City. The same place on the TV.

"Here." The barista held the cordless out. "Lauren," he said sharply, breaking her blurry-eyed trance. Hearing him call her by her name snapped her back to the present. She took the phone and leaned against the counter while his attention turned back to the news.

Her hand shook as she punched in Collin's cell phone number. There was no ring, just a clipping noise before it disconnected. She tried again. And again. She looked helplessly to the barista. "Collin's there," she told him. "His cellular phone just isn't working."

It took a few seconds for the usually attentive barista to realize she was saying something—to him. "Are you okay?" he asked, catching onto her fear and shock.

"My boyfriend is there!" she exclaimed, startling a few people around her.

The barista put his hand over hers on the counter. "Are you sure?"

By this time the inner circle of patrons around her were interested in their exchange. "He left Friday for a reunion with his Marine Corps buddies. He's supposed to fly home tomorrow."

The older golfer next to her removed his ball cap and covered his heart. "Does he have a cellular phone?" he inquired.

"Yes."

The barista's hand remained over hers. His thumb caressed her hand.

"It's not working. I don't know where he was supposed to be today." She pulled her hand back and folded her arms across her chest. The fatherly man next to her seemed a better choice for comfort. "How are we supposed to know if people are okay there? How can I find out where he is and if he's okay?"

The older man continued to hold his hat. "No one knows yet. There's no rulebook on how the US will deal with this on the ground, or abroad. We don't even know exactly who did this yet."

Anger bubbled up in her, for Lauren could not grasp that the government wouldn't know what to do at this point. It was incomprehensible that the systems set in place to deal with disasters were failing her. The unknowing was too much to bear and when the woman on her other side began to fire off questions about Collin, claustrophobia closed in on Lauren. She backed away from the counter as the barista looked to her with a concerned expression. She bolted out the door.

She was panting from running the whole way home. Once inside, her hands dropped to her knees and she doubled over, gasping for air. Her body protested the burst of aerobic activity with sharp side cramps. The discomfort did nothing to alleviate the helplessness she felt. Just as she imagined the rest of the world was doing, she turned on the TV and waited.

Where is he?

As unlikely as it was, she studied every movement in the crowds behind any reporter. Maybe she'd see him.

By midday, she gave up on Collin's number and called Tyler.

"D…" she began after the beep. "Collin, he's in New York right now, the city, and I can't get a hold of him on his cellular phone. I don't know what to do and just really need to hear your voice. Please call me when you get this." Frustration from having no one to talk to caused her to imagine that Thom would probably erase the message.

After another hour of fretting, she threw some clothes in a bag, and got on the 10 heading west.

"Didn't you get my message?" Lauren spoke into the speaker at the gate. Tyler sounded like he'd just woken up. It was shortly after midnight when she pulled up to his exclusive neighborhood. She was edgy, bordering on irritable, because she hadn't stopped to pee the whole way there. Her voice was scratchy as if she had been crying.

"No, what's going on?"

"Can you buzz me in?"

"You're here?"

"Look at your monitor!"

"Jesus, meet me out front, I'll wait outside." A loud buzz preceded the opening of the swirly, wrought iron gates.

She stiffly stood up from the car and ran to give him a quick hug. Oblivious to the lack of lights and closed front door, she started up the front steps. "I didn't stop the whole way here. I really have to pee."

"Thom's asleep." Tyler tried to catch her arm.

"I'll be quiet."

He shot in front of her and opened the door quietly. Once he shut her away in their guest bathroom—with a strict order to stay there—he ran back out to retrieve her bag.

A moment later, Lauren jumped from the sound of something creating a loud thud on tile flooring.

"What are you doing?" Thom called out from the couch.

Shit....

Might as well pull the Band-Aid off, she figured and went back into the foyer. Tyler was rolling in her suitcase as Thom appeared at the same moment. Lauren made the first move and stepped to the suitcase. "I would have gotten that, Tyler."

"Can you just give us a moment, Lauren?" Tyler snapped as he thrust the suitcase toward her.

She huffed off and Thom shot after her, flipping on all the lights as he went.

"What are you doing? Showing up here in the middle of the night?" Thom demanded. "After everything that's going on today? What is going through that daft head of yours?"

Tyler brought up the rear behind Thom and the three of them squared off to each other in the immaculate ivory toned guest quarters that anyone would've paid handsomely for a night's stay...if Casa Fabulous was a B & B.

"Didn't you get any of my messages? Collin's in New York right now. I can't get a hold of him. I don't know what to do. I...I don't know...." The tough exterior that she was trying to maintain began to crumble as her eyes watered and darted from Tyler to Thom. "I don't have anyone else to turn to."

Both men paused at that, even Thom looked sympathetic. Lauren scooped up her suitcase and plopped it on the bed.

Thom shot Tyler a look so scathing that Tyler didn't need to see it to feel its force.

"Just for a few days?" Lauren unzipped her suitcase. "Has your phone service been out, too? Is that why you didn't get my messages?" she directed to Tyler as the lid of her suitcase flopped open.

Tyler wasn't paying attention to her; his focus was diverted to Thom, who looked as though he'd just gone from zero to one hundred.

Four.

"They say all communications are overwhelmed in and around New York." She kept rambling as she took out a toiletries bag and sat on the bed, hoping to pacify whatever was going on with Thom.

Three.

"The rational side of me says he's probably okay...."

Two.

"But the not knowing...and all those people...it's so...."

One.

"All the dirt on the outside of your fucking suitcase is all over the Damask duvet now. There's a luggage stand at the foot of the bed for a reason!"

Blast off!

"What?" She hadn't caught the meaning of what Thom had just said.

Thom grabbed the open suitcase and all but threw it on the luggage stand. "You can't bring all your baggage in and get everything all dirty for him to clean up." He stormed out, leaving Tyler to show her how to work the remote and adjust the thermostat.

The chrome luggage stand set up at the foot of the bed gleamed, like it had never been used.

"I got on his case for the same..." Tyler started and then shrugged. "Never mind, get some sleep."

The next morning, they were both gone. Tyler left a note with instructions to walk Sophie and sign for a package if it came. No one was sure if anything was going to resume or not. They brought home Thai carryout for dinner and the two of them ate in front of the TV while she ate on the deck. Collin's phone still didn't have service.

Another couple of days went by with the TV as the ever present fourth person in the house. Thom had an early morning show guest appearance on Friday to promote the Pura empire. Lauren waited until she thought he was gone, but stopped short of rounding the corner into the kitchen for coffee to hear his voice quavering.

"I don't know if it's cancelled, I don't care. I just need to get out for a bit."

There was a mutter that she couldn't decipher.

Thom sounded like he was scolding Tyler. "We talked about this. I told you I wouldn't stay if you continued to let her take advantage of you. We're supposed to be making something here, something that's ours, and you know we can't do that if you're constantly at her beck and call!"

"Do you understand that he might be dead?" Tyler asked.

"Do you understand it will always be something with her?"

Lauren slumped with guilt. There had always been real love and potential for a long-term relationship between Tyler and Thom. They complemented each other in business and at home, but this was the same fight they'd had too many times to count. Tyler tried to hide it from her for years now. Even so, she was painfully aware of the friction she caused between them.

It ended with an ultimatum. "She better not be here when I come home tonight. You can leave with her if she is."

Lauren crept back to the guest room and packed her things. When she heard the timer indicating the coffee pot was off, she came out with a stretch and a yawn.

"I can make a fresh pot," Tyler offered.

"Don't bother, this is fine."

They kept the conversation on the surface over breakfast and took Sophie for a walk afterwards. It was overcast and gloomy, just like her spirits…still no word from Collin.

"He's not the only one without service," Tyler reminded her. "The flights are just starting back up; it could be days before he gets a seat on one. And the only number he has for you is his house, your home. He might be trying to call you."

"I've called the machine every hour since I've been here. There's only been a few messages from people looking for him."

"He'll be back. Lauren, there's been a terrorist attack on US soil, the magnitude of which no one of our generation has ever experienced. It's going to take a while for people to reunite with each other. He's a Marine, he was in Brooklyn for God's sake, he's just trying to make it to somewhere with service so he can call you and let you know how he's getting home. But you need to be there to get the call, dear."

They stopped under a tree on the trail and Sophie took a shit. Lauren contemplated everything he told her.

"Does Thom hate me?" she finally asked.

"Thom doesn't hate you, but you need to remember, Aimee's his pet. And she never got over you and Collin."

Lauren rolled her eyes at that old drama.

"I know, I know, but still…have some respect for their relationship. And ours. Collin will take care of you. You can't run away every time things get shaky. He'll need you there when he gets home, Lauren. We were on the West Coast when this all happened, but he was a mile away from it. Think about that."

She bagged up the shit and tossed it in the public trash can. "I think he's the one, but you never know, right? I've never thought about marriage, but if I had to imagine having a husband, it would be him. Would you be the one to walk me down the aisle if we got married?"

Tyler laughed at her melodramatic statement. "I'll always be here for you, but I promise you, *this* will be the hardest thing you'll ever have to go through. Well, no, I take that back. When you and Collin have a baby or two, I'll hire you a Swedish nanny, she won't be as hot as you of course."

They laughed and resumed the path to the house.

"Thom and I are in a very precarious place right now, this isn't helping."

"I know, I just thought...."

He patted her shoulder. "I know, hon. It's okay, but we need to figure something out here. Why don't you want to go back? Exactly?"

"It's scary, being there alone. Not knowing where he is, if he's coming home. I don't like being in his house all by myself. No one from the old group is left to hang out with. I must sound so stupid."

"Don't call yourself stupid. Everyone is dealing with this. People are scared and looking for answers. Vegas has run its course for you, that's all. Collin's good for you and like I said, he'll need you to be there when he gets back. Think about what it would be like for him, coming home from God-knows-what to an empty home, girlfriend gone."

Lauren didn't have a response to that and began to tear up.

"You're all grown up now, there's no need for me to watch over your every move anymore. Thom and I are building our dreams here. Do you understand what I'm saying?"

She avoided eye contact with him. Tyler was breaking up with her.

When they returned to the house, she didn't linger.

The last thing Tyler said was, "Don't be a stranger, Lauren."

They both knew it was a lie.

chapter fifteen

East Coast
9/11

Five of the eight hungover Marines navigated their way from Brooklyn to Manhattan at an ungodly hour in the morning on Tuesday, September 11, 2001. Attending a 9:00 a.m. breakfast hosted by the Quartermaster from VFW Post 528 in a restaurant located in the iconic "Windows on the World" complex seemed like a good idea…Saturday afternoon. But that was before the weekend turned a corner and went down the road of glory days' past.

Mayhem kicked Collin's shoe a moment before their subway stop. "Good thing you brought your stunt liver," he joked to Collin's blurry eyes. "Don't worry, there'll be Bloody Marys."

A sharp blast of cold air caused Collin's adrenaline to snap to attention; as did the sea of people moving in all directions that started on the subway platform. Swimming upstream though the crowd wasn't natural for any of them. They might as well have had the word TOURISTS blinking in flashing lights over their heads.

Still, they managed to make it to the entrance of the North Tower with time to spare—8:40 a.m. to be exact—as Collin pulled out a pack of cigarettes. All but Mayhem had no desire to waste time with a quick smoke before breakfast. "We'll be up on the next elevator," Collin promised as the other Marines rushed in to find the elevators that went up to the 106th floor.

"Do you still want to see Stephanie?" Mayhem asked while the two stood under the awning shading the main entrance of the building.

"It's not a matter of what I want, it's a matter of what's right. I've got a swab kit with me and if she won't have Charles submit a sample, then I'm done. I can't hold onto her anymore." He took a drag and through a steady stream of smoke, he muttered, "I'll go crazy if I do."

Mayhem nodded and stubbed out his cigarette. "Let's go."

The blast and vibration that shook for the next seconds caused Collin to experience something akin to an out of body experience. Screams, confusion, and chaos rapidly came to a boil and from high above he saw himself pushing people out of the way to keep up with Mayhem hightailing it into the lobby.

Someone smacked into them. "You're going the wrong way!" the man shouted in a panic.

Mayhem grabbed Collin before he tripped and hollered, "Grover, c'mon, our brothers! Leave no man behind!" with an "Ooh Rah!" to boot.

Moving upstream through the subway platform crowd less than an hour ago, was a hot knife through butter compared to navigating their way through the chaos in the lobby. But Mayhem was a force, pulling people out of the way as the two men followed the same path their fellow Marines would have gone to reach the correct elevator bank. Collin struggled to match Mayhem's speed and intensity.

Another explosion.

Collin wiped ash from the face of his watch.

9:03 a.m.

Finally, the elevators were in sight behind the wall of bodies bursting from the stairwell doors. A machine with a singular focus, Mayhem shoved through the mob toward the stairs with Collin on his tail. The fight became a game of stop and start. Their mission turned from finding their friends, to assisting fleeing people. The outpouring of horrified expressions didn't let up and the passage of time became indiscernible. Collin would later learn that they had remained in that stairwell landing for just under an hour pulling people out, helping them up, and pushing them on toward safety.

When an earthshattering thunder caused everything to shake for longer than a quick burst, Collin knew things were breaking down. Calculating that there wasn't much time left to get out of the North Tower before an avalanche of concrete, steel, and bodies would trap them, he made the final push to reach Mayhem further up the stairwell. He'd drag his best friend out if needed.

Within seconds, everything changed when he saw Mayhem, a limp body barely propped up on the shoulders between two civilians. "What the fuck happened?" Collin cried.

"People panicked at that last explosion, he was caught under them!" the man shouted. The pair let him collapse onto Collin's strong frame in the mess of all souls running for their lives. Blood ran down Collin's chest as he hoisted Mayhem up over his shoulder. There was no time to be gentle and one of his arms dangled in a disturbing manner while being further banged up as they descended the stairwell. He knew it, in his gut, that Mayhem had been crushed.

After backtracking through the entrance of the complex, Collin wondered if he was carrying a corpse. Several pieces of broken building blocked their path to possible safety and Collin stumbled around as they made it to the ash-covered street.

This was the war we trained for.

With visibility near zero, Collin was unable to determine how far they made it past the last barricade. Two blocks? Three?

As far as a line charge would shoot?

Both men hit the ground among a mess of carnage and inescapable noise. Collin grappled at some medics performing triage. They were blurred figures, like angels shifting through dust. "My buddy! I need a medic!" A sharp tug on his pant leg caused Collin to look down and see Mayhem's eyes open. Collin dropped to his knees as the sensation of time suspending under a peaceful blanket covered them. His hands captured the sides of Mayhem's skull to steady it; it was impossible to determine if his spinal cord had been damaged.

"It wasn't me," Mayhem's voice croaked.

Tears emerged from every orifice of Collin's entire being.

"The line charge," he wheezed, "it wasn't me...the fuse didn't light, my ignitor failed...."

"What are you talking about?"

"In Kuwait, it was an angel."

"What? You're not making sense, man."

"That fuse didn't light, my ignitor failed...."

"What? An angel?"

"There was an angel there; she looked like the chick with no gag reflex in Oceanside." Mayhem couldn't hold back a shit eating grin. "I swear man, it wasn't me who primed that second line charge, my ignitor was toast. The angel did it."

"No, man, it blew. You did it, we all saw you…." The tears, they wouldn't stop. "Runnin' like a bat outta hell."

Collin pulled Mayhem's head into his chest and kissed his forehead and cheeks, insisting that he'd be okay. "The medics said they'd be right back, just hold on!"

"Grover, listen to me! He's not yours, the test…it was done years ago, I'm so sorry…I should've told you."

"It's okay, just—" The North Tower began to fall as did Collin's world. "You don't know that. Just…just hold on!"

"Donna told me, he's Dan's." Mayhem's eyes unexpectedly lit up as they bore into Collin's with relief and joy. "She's your curse, man. Go back to Vegas and love that sweet girlfriend of yours, you lucky son of a bitch. Forget Steph." His smile—the same one that preceded every scheme they'd ever embarked upon from forever ago—that smile spread across his face, where it remained intact until his body was cremated.

The days of dealing with the aftermath from being stuck at ground zero turned into a week. Then two. At first, there was no cell phone signal, no way to call out on a landline, and all public transportation had come to a standstill. After several days of helping with the rescue efforts, Collin's body and mind couldn't handle any more exposure.

Grief was in every face at every turn. While staying with Donna in Jersey, he witnessed the sassy party girl shrink, gray, and age at a rapid pace.

"When did she tell you?" he asked the morning before he was set to leave. His back was toward her as he stared at the urn on her mantle over the fireplace.

Mayhem.

"When you got out. She thought you'd come home, not go to Vegas."

"Did you see the test results?"

"No, like I said, she just told me that he was Dan's. I didn't say anything to Mayhem about it 'til after we came to visit you in February. I figured he'd tell you, you know, so you wouldn't have it hanging over your head now that you're with her." A pause. "Have you called her yet?"

He bypassed the topic of Lauren and turned around to face Donna. "Do you believe her?"

She shrugged. "You know how she is."

He did. Stephanie was just the type who'd keep him and Dan strung along for years. Once the mind-blowing sex cooled, she'd turn to the irresistible bait of her son, Charles. Born the first of November in 1991, the possibility of him being Collin's son was high. Equally as high was the possibility that Dan was his father. Now, with Mayhem's car and a long drive back to Vegas, there remained just one last stop before heading west.

He figured that he'd be able to tell if the boy was his just by looking at him... *right?* And now he was less than an hour from laying eyes on the kid. But seeing wasn't enough and for all these years, Steph had been the only thing standing in the way of getting the inside of Charles's cheek swabbed. This was the final bid Collin would make for the paternity test. He was not going to be strung along anymore.

As the bridge became smaller in his rearview mirror, Collin thought of Lauren, wondering how she was doing with the news of the terrorist attack. He pictured her spectacular breasts hanging over him when she rode him in the middle of the day. She didn't mind if he left the curtains open so the sunlight would hit her. She was good about letting him look at her when they had sex, there was no inhibition. But he reminded himself that she was young and all that would eventually be replaced with the once-per-week missionary style under the covers. And that would probably happen sooner rather than later if he brought a ten-year-old boy back to Vegas with him.

Does she even want kids?

But then again, sometimes she surprised him. When he'd arrived to Brooklyn and unpacked, there was a copy of Ayn Rand's *The Fountainhead* stowed away in his bag. Stuck to the inside flap was a yellow Post-it note: *In case you forgot reading material for the plane.* No flowery hearts or even her name to mark her territory. He wondered if she wanted to give him the option to take out the note and pitch it. He also wondered if she would pack up and leave Las Vegas once she graduated.

Or pack up and leave him.

It was hard to judge if she was satisfied with their quiet lifestyle. Her social life had come to a standstill and her only real outings these days were yoga classes.

He discreetly cringed when she mentioned those classes. His mom predicted that she might grow out of this hippie-dippy, new-age phase. "She's only twenty-one for God's sake, Collin," she sighed in exasperation over the phone a few weeks back. She hadn't met Lauren in person yet. When she did, he hoped that his mom would see Lauren's depth.

Yoga classes or not, it was better than spending her days at a park, absently pushing a couple of kids on swings while gossiping with the other wives living on base. Chain smoking menthols—that's what they did.

Those girls wouldn't like her, most didn't. The recollection of Donna calling her a "fag hag" crossed his mind as he lit another cigarette. Stephanie, on the other hand, loved that shit. She held court with those broads and could always be counted on to bum smokes. She never bought any herself.

The exit came up faster than anticipated.

Collin checked for phone service one last time while stopped a block down from her house. Subconsciously, he wanted to warn her with the futile hope of not being blindsided by Dan answering the door. Service hadn't been restored and he walked down her block in the amount of time it took him to finish two cigarettes.

When her front door opened, he stepped back to make sure he had the house number correct. "Dan? Jesus, I didn't recognize you."

The guy extended his hand. "Mike."

It had been three weeks since the attack, when he finally made it back to his place in Las Vegas. Collin was surprised to see a sizable American flag hung off a pole by the front door. It was sturdily attached to the siding. When the breeze caught it, he paused to admire it. The moment of pride was immediately shadowed by suspicion when he inspected the brackets. They were screwed in tight and lined up evenly with the door frame. No way Lauren put this up.

He entered quietly and set down his bags. The condo was immaculate. All her boxes that had littered the living room over the summer were gone and the faint smell of Pine-Sol emanated from the kitchen. He didn't call out for her. He promised himself that this would be the one and only time he'd put her fidelity to the test. If she passed, he'd ask her to marry him. If not, then goodbye to another slut.

There was music coming from their bedroom, it was muffled, like the door was shut. The Eagles. "Take it Easy"? It wasn't even something she would listen to.... His guard skyrocketed as he crept up the stairs. Someone else must have gone through his CDs and had the audacity to play them in his bedroom. Jealousy caused his vision to tunnel as he scanned the hallway leading to his master bedroom, looking for signs of another man. The door was shut and he could hear Don Henley crooning about a girl while his own heart raced and his anger brewed to a rage.

The St. Germain curse began with his grandmother: not waiting for her husband when he returned to their French village after years of imprisonment during WWII. His own mother, Nadine: tormenting his father by acting out on her insatiable need for male attention. When his dad caught wind of his son eyeing the girls in the neighborhood, he laid it down for a fourteen-year-old Collin.

"Don't let those manipulative little creatures into your head. You know what'll happen." The warning haunted every bid he made for a girlfriend throughout his teen years.

Driving thousands of miles over the past few days with no one to talk to but himself, he concluded that he had just dodged a bullet in New Jersey. Convinced that he outsmarted the curse by cutting ties with Stephanie, he was ready to embrace Lauren.

But the closed bedroom door muting the blaring music degraded his newfound optimism. The trust in Lauren he'd idealized during his road trip? Down the drain. His hand squeezed the bedroom doorknob as images of all the unfaithful women from his past blended together to form a vision of Lauren in his head. In it, she'd morphed into the archetype to which all St. Germain men were bound: the Lolita. Iblis smiled in satisfaction from her side.

He shook his head, but it didn't make the hallucination go away. He was just about to bang his head on the wall when the unmistakable groan of furniture being rocked came from behind the door. Suddenly, everything came into focus.

Red focus.

He flung open the door, instantly opening up the volume to bombard his senses.

Lauren was kneeling next to his side of the bed when Collin burst in. She was in a precarious position, half-holding herself over the corner of his heavy nightstand with one hand while the other was curved around the back reaching for something. She gasped and lost her balance. Her head clipped the sharp corner of his nightstand with a loud smack.

Still uncertain if someone else was in the room, Collin flew over as she scrambled to get up and confront the intruder. Blood streamed into her eye.

"Collin!" she wailed in relief while at the same time pushing him away with a punch in the chest. She was a mess of blood, sweat, and frizzy hair from cleaning.

He trapped her wrists and engulfed her while scanning the room. She was alone.

Jesus, what have I done?

Blinded by an ooze of red and unmatched to his strength, she collapsed, sobbing.

He inspected her face and used his shirt sleeve to wipe away some blood. It was a split. "I am so, so sorry, honey, I didn't mean to startle you. C'mon…." He tried to lead her to the bathroom.

"What?!" She hiccupped as she fought to breath. "Where have you been? Why didn't you call me? I was so…." She strained to speak. "How did you get home?

Why didn't you call me?!" The hiccups overtook her and blood dripped onto the bedspread, but her feet remained firmly planted on the ground.

"Calm down. I know, let's get this bleeding under control and I'll tell you everything. Are you okay?"

She wiggled out of his grip and covered her eyes.

Collin gently smoothed her hair back and kissed the top of her head. "It's okay," he cooed. "I'm here, I'll never leave you again. I love you and there's nothing that could keep me from you, I promise."

He turned down the stereo while she went into the bathroom to clean the cut. He took one more look around, the room was spotless with the exception of her fresh blood staining the bedspread. He grabbed a first aid kit from the closet. It was still neatly packed away in the survival box she made for their camping trip.

"Sit down on the edge of the tub. Keep your head up." He pulled out butterfly sutures.

She held a wet washcloth on the swelling temple. "Where have you been?"

"Shhh, just hold on." He painstakingly peeled the bandage from its wrapper.

"Why didn't you call me?" The hiccups slowed, but one still broke the million-dollar question in two. The washcloth dropped as she made an effort to glare up at him.

"No, no." he tempered as if she was a little girl. "Sit back, honey. Please." He sunk to his knees and guided her hand back to the injury. "Keep pressure with the wash cloth, okay? Just relax, baby, and let me fix you. I'll tell you everything—I promise—but for now, we've gotta get this bleeding to stop."

She finally calmed down and he bandaged her wound with the utmost of care.

His lips lingered in a gentle kiss on her temple. "What were you doing on my side of the bed?" he asked softly.

"Unplugging your alarm clock. I wanted to use it on my side."

His eyes closed and a faint smile appeared. "Why were you listening to The Eagles?"

"I thought you might like it if we had some music in common."

It was that sweet, but simple, statement that released a low hum of laughter from his throat. Relief was short-lived, though, and submitted to a choking noise coming from his chest. Gasping sobs came next as he slumped into her breasts. He didn't know if she was shocked, re-pulsed, or both at the sight of him breaking down and bawling like a child on her. Perhaps neither, because she didn't hesitate to draw him into her warmth. Her lips were on his head, soft pecks with murmurs of comfort in between.

So much time had passed that his legs fell asleep and her chest was raw from his unshaven face. "Honey, Mayhem…he died in the attack. They all did."

Her wide eyes displayed the horror anyone would experience upon receiving that news. But her face…it was the face of a toddler who cried every night in hopes that a father would come home. It was that face that was bared to him by the woman sitting on the edge of his bathtub.

"I lost them all. I can't lose you, too," Collin confessed.

chapter sixteen

Officially Collin and Lauren's Place
CHRISTMAS EVE, 2001

"I love that we finally have a fire pit back here," Lauren repeated as she plopped down with a Diet Coke.

"Yeah," Collin absently responded as he pulled the other chair closer to hers. He cracked open a beer with his free hand.

"What's in the box?"

"Some old photos I found cleaning out the closet. Thought you'd like to look through them."

The evening air still carried enough light for her to make out the black and white images on fading backgrounds.

"This was my grandfather, Jean-Claude St. Germain. He was a prisoner of war in Germany." The man in the photo possessed traces of Collin, especially around the eyes and brow.

"They posed with such formality," Lauren remarked as she carefully thumbed through a few photos. "He was a captain, like you?"

"No, I was a Corporal, it's different, remember?"

Lauren set the box aside and scooted closer. "So, your full name is Collin Andrew St. Germain." She smiled expectantly.

"Miss James, your last name will sound pretty much the same, you know, just with a 'St.' in front of it."

"Do you ever spell out the 'St.' part? Like is it officially 'Saint Germain,' but everyone just abbreviates it?"

"Not unless you're an ascended master."

"Huh?"

"Sorry, old family joke, seriously though, no one spells it all the way out. Even on my DD214. Hold on a sec, I need another beer. Want anything?"

Lauren shook her head.

He returned with two beers and a smoke. It was a typical Collin campfire story in the making. "Grab the box."

Lauren stowed it on her lap, untied her hair, and arranged herself so that her best angles faced him. The intent to steer the conversation off dusty relics and onto one that led to the bedroom was on her mind.

Mimicking his father's voice, Collin began, "St. Germain family legend has it that every male born with the surname will be cursed by a race of ancient and powerful beings, the djinn, son, don't forget." Collin paused for a swig of beer and his voice returned to normal. "Supposedly, my grandfather spoiled the plans of their most revered leader, Iblis, during World War Two."

The air between them was dark for a moment; until he goosed her and she jumped with a short yelp. "Collin! You're shitting me!"

His head dropped back and he laughed. "Did you know that the word gullible isn't in the dictionary?"

She tried to act offended, but he was in such a good mood that she couldn't help but to be drawn into him. *We're back*, she decided. Everything between them was comfortable and easy again. It had been a tense couple of months since he returned from New York.

"I know you said the ring was fine, but you should really have this." His hand slid onto her lap, pausing at the dip between her legs, before retrieving the box. Under the stack of pictures was a sizable sapphire set in a vintage ring, encased by lavish, intricate platinum curves. It was feminine, sophisticated, and encrusted in diamond chips that paled as the backdrop for the flawless gem. "It belonged to my grandfather's third wife. She was from North Africa, and it's never been worn by any other woman."

Lauren's right hand cupped her mouth as her jaw dropped. A piece of obvious luxury, it made her think of some fancy jeweler saying, *"It's absolutely stunning,"* in a nasally voice while looking down his nose. Tears of gratitude rimmed her eyelids as he found her left hand and slid off the modest ring he'd purchased on the fly.

"This ring's unique. It was specially crafted to protect the wearer. Not solid platinum or solid gold, it's iron under a platinum coating. Djinn are weakened by iron," he mumbled, almost as an afterthought, and waited until she finished admiring her new engagement ring to continue. "I know it seems like a joke, the curse, but—"

"What?" She cut him off, not caring about some old story, but bubbling over with excitement for her upgraded bling.

"Iblis is real."

Her head reared around to study his expression, trying to discern if this was a continuation in his attempts to tease her. She blinked first. There wasn't a hint of joviainess in his eyes.

"When I was a kid, Iblis—I just called it, well IT, in my head—used to appear in my room at night. My mom chalked it up to night terrors which didn't make things better, so I stopped telling her until she thought the phase was over. IT scared the bejesus out of me until I was old enough to cope with the fear. People in the west think of them as genies, but they're actually called the djinn." He'd been avoiding the word "djinn" for months now and only resorted to calling them by their proper name when he ran out of more palatable synonyms for the word.

Still anticipating the punchline, she pressed her lips together as the need to call bullshit was on the tip of her tongue.

"They say kids are more susceptible to experiencing these types of things because they're not jaded from experience. That's probably why it all faded away after I'd been in the Corps for a while. Finally got to a point when IT wasn't even on my radar anymore."

"Do you think," she started and stopped, trying to figure out what she wanted to ask. It was incredulous that he's never mentioned any of this until now. "Do you think that this…this Iblis entity still haunts you?"

"No." His eyes shifted to the fire so abruptly that she questioned if he was telling the truth.

She snatched up his second beer and raised it. "To Mayhem!"

His half-empty beer can chinked hers. "Yes, to Mayhem. He'd be so proud of you, getting a degree that will benefit national security."

They drank.

"After what happened, to him, to our country, what else could I do?" Lauren trailed off and her own eyes shot to the fire.

chapter seventeen

Las Vegas
JANUARY 2002

"Seriously, Lauren, what do you want to be when you grow up? Tyler's gone, honey. You've only got one more semester. And the money…well that's almost gone, too." Collin struggled to keep calm. It was baffling that the closer she got to her degree the more she'd revert to acting helpless about what to do with it.

"What the hell am I going to do with this stupid Criminal Justice degree? I hate blood!" She pierced the last sentence with sarcasm that begged him to take the bait into an argument. He had lectured her so many times about all the different careers that did not involve blood, or dead bodies, or guns, or any other crazy rationale she came up with to get out of working in the real world. She knew just how to push his buttons, and the blood bit was just the tip of the iceberg.

He threw the tongs down in frustration and marched off to get another cigarette. Lauren took his spot at the grill and plucked up the tongs. From the kitchen window, he watched her poke the chicken breasts with exaggerated calmness. When he reemerged, she moved to the side and offered the handle to him. Smoke in one hand, Maker's in the other; no stories around the campfire tonight—just war time tales. He balanced the cigarette filter off the side of the grill and snatched the tongs from her limp hand.

Her eyes remained glued to the chicken as if it were the most important aspect of the evening.

"We can't afford to stay here unless we both take full-time jobs. Where? On the Strip? You want to go cocktail? You want me to drive to the airport every day? Get on the J Plane?"

He pressed the chicken on the grill, making it unnecessarily sizzle and spray hot juice at them. He was ready for whatever rebuttal she had stored up for this discussion. Even though she was proficient with her arguments, he was still the master at breaking down every idea she presented. He had the ability to turn all her ideas into paths of resistance destined for failure.

"You can stay here to finish up your last semester while I'm away at training. You only have eleven more fucking credits! You can actually do something with a

Criminal Justice degree! Isn't that what you wanted? That's what you said after the attack!"

"My Spanish sucks!"

"No one speaks Spanish on post."

The obvious wheels began turning, no doubt she was considering half a dozen retorts and tossing them aside. This was a rerun of the past few fights between them; she could predict his response to each of them.

Was she finally out of excuses?

He hoped it was accepting defeat that caused her to go inside.

She returned with a Maker's and Diet Coke—her drink whenever she made one.

"Do you want to eat inside or out?" he asked while plating it.

She emptied the glass and lost her edge. "Can we at least go down there together before you accept the job?"

Collin relaxed, the battle had been won. "Why don't we hop on a flight to El Paso tomorrow? We can come back Sunday. I don't have to let them know 'til Monday."

"Andale pues." She motioned toward the door. "It's too cold out here."

With her back to him, he indulged in a victory grin that quickly transformed to the attentive, understanding mask once at the table inside. "Sit down," he offered. "I'll pour you another drink and get the salad." He took his time in the kitchen and typed out a quick text to his friend working for the investigations department.

Collin: *She's on board. Can you contact her soon about the position?*
01/24/2002, 7:01 p.m.

Mike Brown (OPM investigator): *Yep, we need to fill the position NLT May. She's on top of the list.*
01/24/2002, 7:05 p.m.

PART III

FORT BLISS MILITARY COMPLEX

chapter eighteen

Boyers, PA
JULY 2002

"Hello, my name is Lauren St. Germain, Special Investigator retained by the US Office of Personnel Management." She fumbled with her creds, praying that her picture wasn't upside-down as the man behind the desk glanced at them. She wasn't sure if she should wait for him to invite her to sit down. Her feet were killing her and she held out her creds longer than necessary.

"What can I do for you?" No offer to sit. No eye contact.

Lauren's notebook was open and ready. Shuffling the creds, the pen, and Subject's release while standing over him made her look ridiculous, unprofessional. The need to start the source interview was painfully overdue.

"I'm currently working on a background investigation for an Alfonso Ramirez and you're listed as his commanding officer. Are you, uh, busy, I mean available to do a reference interview for him?"

"Well, you're already here," he responded with a stifled sigh. His gaze shifted to one of the chairs across from him and then back down to his paperwork.

It was another minute of pulling two chairs apart, then turning to the side to squeeze between them, and then deciding which one to sit in...all the while dealing with a pen cap (*fuck!*), creds, and a notebook. She muttered, "Okay," and caught herself before she presented her creds again.

Already did that, Lauren, just start the interview already!

"When did you first meet Alfonso Ramirez and by what name do you know him?"

"Private First Class Ramirez, when he arrived to the unit six months ago."

"How often do you see him on average?"

"Every day."

"At, um, work? Or do you socialize with him outside of...." Lauren struggled to find the equivalent of work to military daily activity.

"We serve together in a Staff Sergeant/PFC capacity. There's no socialization between ranks."

"Right, sorry." She wrote 'no social' in her notebook. "Do you know where he lives?"

"No."

She wrote "no resi" before continuing. "Do you know how long he's worked here…err…been in the US military, I mean?"

"He's a PFC, so he's been enlisted in the Army, at the very least, a year. He's been in my unit for six months though. I'm not sure where he was before."

Her pen hoovered over the paper. There was something she needed to recall about assumptions here.

"Investigator St. Germain," he snapped.

Her head shot up. "Um, sorry, so you think he's been in for at least a year. Do you know when he started boot camp?"

He sat back in the chair and told her to put down her notebook. "Take a breather, Lauren, you have to keep the line of questioning consistent with OPM guidelines. You were about to open a can of worms."

She dropped the notebook on the desk and sat back with a huff. This trainer liked to rattle her. "I'm going in the same order that's on the cheat sheet," she protested.

"I know, but I said he's only been serving under me for six months. You can't take someone's estimation about how long his subordinate's been in the army, based on rank. Do you see what I mean? You can only accept first-hand knowledge from a source. You get Subject's start date from his record."

It was incredibly frustrating. She'd been up all night studying her notecards with Geneva, another Investigator-in-Training, in the hotel lobby. They'd practiced mock interviews with each other so they'd smoke this evaluation. She knew that assumptive information was inadmissible. How could she get caught in that at the very beginning of the interview?

She must not have been hiding her frustration very well because the trainer misinterpreted the reason behind her irritation. "That's how they'll talk to you, you have to get used to it."

She met his eyes with determination. "I don't care about that."

He laughed. "Tell you what, why don't you send in the next person. Practice the questions a few times and then come back in for a redo. We'll just call this 'dress rehearsal' and I won't mark a grade on it."

Geneva was next in line.

"He's going to be a dick to you," Lauren warned her. She took the list of questions and went for a walk. She was sick of sitting in the overly air conditioned classroom crammed with all the other trainees. She could practice the interview outside—alone.

Lauren returned an hour later and hopped back in line to do the mock source interview. This time she sat down without being asked and rattled off the Privacy Act of 1974 while flashing her creds for a brief second. The whole interview took twenty minutes, the shortest one in the class.

"That's much better," the trainer told her once they finished.

"I thought it was supposed to take a half an hour, minimum."

"That's what the handbook says, but when you're out in the field, well, let's just say you won't hit your numbers if you take that long with each source. You only need the bare minimum, don't deviate from the required questions. Besides, no source in the world wants you interviewing him for thirty minutes or more. Well..." he looked her up and down, "they might not mind you interviewing them for that long." His grin was goofy, like he was trying to be self-deprecating, but his eyes were hopeful that she might take the bait and flirt back.

The fingers on her left hand drummed the table lightly, her sapphire sparkled.

He cleared his throat as his spine stiffened. The professional, somewhat dismissive, tone came back. "You did pretty well for your first time. Maintain control of the interview. Remember, if they bring anything up, you must resolve it, so don't let them veer off into things that aren't needed. You'll get the hang of it in no time."

"How long does it take to get it right?"

"At least six months on the job, sometimes a year."

Right before graduating in June of 2002 with that CRJ degree, she'd been recruited by a government contractor to take a federal investigator position. Her badge was contingent upon two things: graduation (*duh*), and that she pass a rigorous background investigation finding her suitable to obtain and maintain a Top Secret security clearance. (*Miraculously, that did happen*).

She had no qualms about her ability to succeed in her new position. She scored almost perfect marks during training and left for El Paso with badge in hand.

c h a p t e r   n i n e t e e n

Al Aeropuerto Internacional de El Paso, Tejas
BIENVENIDO

The following month Collin stood at the bottom of the escalator with a bouquet of roses he'd just purchased from the self-service flower machine a few yards away. He tucked a small American flag in it. They hadn't seen each other in over a month and he felt that starting this chapter of their life together was going to be the start of their legacy.

He complimented her new hairstyle first thing. "It's very sleek," he said as he palmed the side of it. Pin straight, shiny hair curled in at the top of her shoulder. "You look so professional, Mrs. St. Germain. Or should I say Special Investigator St. Germain?"

Collin had been working as an IED specialist for Booz Allen Hamilton since February. When she came down in July, they found a sizable track home on a cul-

de-sac in the northeast part of El Paso where all the soldiers lived—it was brand new construction. While she
was training in Pennsylvania, he took it upon himself to
finance all new furniture as a surprise. He really wanted
the house to be nice for Lauren when she arrived. Convinced that if her physical surroundings were new, he anticipated that she'd be just as happy there as she was in
Vegas.

While waiting for her luggage, she showed him a
brand-new Nokia cell phone that was issued to her for
work.

"I can use it for personal use, too. They don't want
us carrying two phones even though they can't prohibit
it. What's cool about this one is that it has GPS, too."

He smiled as he messed around with the shiny new
screen on it. There had been talk about Booz issuing cell
phones sometime in the near future, but as with all things
that add to the budget, it was still in discussion. When
she held out her hand for it back, he gave it to her with
reluctance. He'd play around with it later.

"How does some authentic Mexican food for dinner
sound?" he asked once they were in his truck on the way
home.

"Sure," she replied. "It looks pretty much like Vegas
here. Desert is desert, don't you think?"

"This is high desert. The elevation here is almost
4,000 feet."

She continued to look out the window at the sea of brown.

"I have a surprise for you at home." he tried. He hadn't meant to correct her before, but it just came out.

"Is it a puppy?" When she faced him, the brilliant smile he'd missed, it lit up her face.

"Two, I didn't want him to be lonely."

"Oh boy...." She chuckled.

Lauren's back was to him as she entered their house, so he couldn't gage her initial reaction. When he stepped up to her, he was relieved to see a joyous awe splashed all over her face. It was genuine. He knew he was right to bypass his coworker's wife's offer to pick out the décor. "Wait 'til you see the bedroom."

She squealed in delight and scampered off to the master. She made it up there before he had time to set down her suitcases and close the front door. "Collin!" she hollered from upstairs. "Oh, my God! This is gorgeous!" Her face poked over the railing. "This is just too much, but oh, I love it!"

Collin ran up after her as she shot back into their room and flopped down on the king-sized bed like an angel, causing the down comforter to make a poof-like noise. It was chocolate brown and it felt like soft suede, perfect for her to cuddle up in completely naked. Her exposed leg with a sandal dangling off her toe was even softer than the bedspread. The sandal dropped to the stone-colored shag carpet, barely a muffled knock on the ground. Her leg curled around him and she yanked him off balance so he had no choice to fall directly on her.

God, she feels good.

Like a puppy, she wiggled under him and kissed him all over his face. As the other sandal dropped to the floor, her pecks slowed and her lips found his. The moan that escaped her throat was such a relief to him, she hadn't changed completely.

"Don't you want to check out the bathroom?" he asked with benignity, even though his mouth pressed into her neck and his erection drove into her waist.

"Not really, not now. I have missed you…this…." Her hands took no time to glide under the bottom of his shirt and pressed her palms into the small of his back. It was slick with sweat and her fingertips slipped as she clasped his torso.

Half-laughing with urgency, they hopped up and tore their own clothes off. In a moment of manic inhibition, she flung all the bedding back to expose the sheets. The action reminded him of the glitter bomb that went off the first time he laid eyes on her. The throw pillows he'd agonized over a few hours ago, tumbled down and the scent of Downy was released.

The creamy, ivory, jacquard sheets were the highest thread count he could find. Her eyes widened and then became wickedly sexy. "Oh, Collin!" she exclaimed and sprawled out on the bed. No panties, no bra, just her bare skin that was warm to his touch.

He eased down on top of her and kissed a trail down her chest while she grasped his hair. Her spine arched as he captured one nipple with his teeth. His tongue throbbed against it and his hand caught the other one. Kneading into her soft flesh was intoxicating. Her legs parted and the dampness between them pressed against his thigh. He let loose and took to her cleft with his mouth while his hands remained busy on her breasts. When his tongue found her clit, and flicked it, she reacted as if she'd just received an electric shock. Her thighs clenched so hard they trembled. He palmed her sex. "Shhh…just relax. Enjoy."

Before he dipped back down between her legs, he looked up and watched as her head rotated from side to side. Her perfectly coiffed hair stuck to the bed, rumpling out the last bit of Special Investigator St. Germain.

c h a p t e r   t w e n t y

El Paso, Texas
SPRING 2005

Lauren was excited. Like so excited that she couldn't focus on the report she was typing up right in front of her. Geneva was coming TDY to El Paso for the next month.

It wasn't because Lauren was drowning in cases due to staffing shortages. It wasn't even because she'd finally be able to take a week off work since another "seasoned" investigator would be down there picking up some of the slack. It was because she hadn't hung out with anyone other than Collin and his work buddies in what felt like forever. Throwing herself into overtime brought her much success as an investigator, but there was no balance in her life. No yoga. No gay "husbands." No girl-friends. Not even any work events that could be considered remotely social.

Ever since they met in training, Lauren and Geneva continued to stay in touch, bemoaning over cases, deadlines, OPM guidelines, reviews, and eventually, lack of satisfaction in their careers, lives, bodies, husbands.... Going through the same bureaucratic nightmare that was the security clearance world had bonded them. They e-mailed or texted, but rarely spoke on the phone, except for when Geneva called to tell Lauren she was coming down there to work. It had been almost three years since they'd seen each other in person.

Thoughts of driving Geneva around the first day or two so she could get her bearings teased Lauren to fantasize about going out for happy hour with a girlfriend once 5:00 p.m. hit. She wanted to talk, in English, for hours and hours with someone who understood this job. Someone who didn't think Collin was a national treasure. Someone who would check out cute guys and giggle profusely at getting caught.

Lauren wanted to think of Geneva as being Tyler reincarnated, but that was projecting. A phrase she'd become quite familiar with lately. It was the end all be all response to anything she ever brought up with Collin.

"I wish you'd cancel on them, just this week. We could go on a hike, maybe dinner after?" It was a hopeful notion that he'd cancel Wednesday: "Guys' Night."

"I don't know why you set yourself up to get hurt. You know Wednesdays are my night to go out with my friends."

"Is it because you don't want to spend time with me?"

His sigh was heavy. *"This isn't about you, Lauren, stop projecting."*

Sunday afternoons were out of bounds as well because that's when all the "guys" went shooting at the Fort Bliss Rod and Gun Club. The pattern of their weeks was set early on and hadn't changed over the past three years. Almost three years, anyway.

But for one glorious month in 2005, Lauren was elated that he'd be off doing his thing. Now, if she could only wish away the constant dust storms that were inevitable during April and May, life would be pretty darn close to perfect.

"When you get assigned something at Fort Bliss, it's usually on the post proper, but not always. Bliss is probably the most heavily funded military complex in the US. So, it includes McGregor Range, Wizzmer, and Tobin Wells. Some of that is in New Mexico even though it says Fort Bliss on the case." Lauren pulled up to the Pershing Gate and rolled down her window. "Do you have your creds out?" she asked Geneva.

"Yep."

In a smooth motion, Lauren flipped both sets of creds open to the soldier. He didn't reach for their creds, as most soldiers knew they couldn't touch any badge presented as ID to enter Fort Bliss. He looked past Lauren at Geneva. "Two of you today?"

"She's here TDY, just showing her what's what," Lauren explained.

The gate lifted and Lauren glanced over to Geneva, not sure if she was talking too much during their first morning together. Geneva didn't seem interested in what she had to say and continued to thumb through some paperwork on her lap in the passenger seat.

"This gate is only open from oh-seven-hundred 'til, like," Lauren found it difficult to talk to her friend in person, "...um, sixteen-hundred. It's really only supposed to be for the residents, but we can...we can go through whatever gate we want."

"'Kay." Geneva didn't look up. After a moment, she asked, "Wizzmer?"

"White Sands Missile Range, W, S, M, R. Wizzmer. There's also the national park side to it. We could go, if you like, and see the sand dunes. It's beautiful, like being on another planet."

"Uh-huh."

The rest of the day was altogether uncomfortable. Lauren finally resolved herself to the uneasy silence between them. When she took Geneva to pick up a rental car at the end of the day, Lauren chanced one more attempt to connect. "Do you want to maybe get together for lunch or something? Once you're all settled in, I mean."

"Sure, great." Geneva shut the door and walked off carrying an armful of cases while pulling a rolling computer bag that wobbled behind her. Geneva had gained a considerable amount of weight since they last saw each other, causing her to struggle to keep up with Lauren's fast pace all day.

Once Lauren realized that Geneva was gasping for air by the time they reached a building entrance, she purposefully slowed her gait. It might have been too late, though, and Lauren wondered if Geneva resented her for it. It was almost as if the insinuation that they needed to walk slower due to Geneva's fitness level was a cruel thing to do in and of itself.

Lauren was pleasantly surprised and relieved to get a few friendly texts from Geneva over the next several days. Then, on Saturday morning, she was downright thrilled when this pinged her phone.

Geneva: *Want to go out for some drinks tonight? Need to blow off some STEAM.*
04/30/2005, 4:00 p.m.

Lauren hesitated—if she responded too quickly, she'd seem desperate. Before Geneva arrived, she wouldn't have thought twice about instantly texting back, but now she was overanalyzing the situation. She finished up the last few lines on her report, scanned it, and then went back to her phone.

Lauren: *Sure, anything specific in mind?*
04/30/2005, 4:12 p.m.

Geneva: *Anywhere with lots of hot, drunk soldiers.*
04/30/2005, 4:13 p.m.

Geneva: *J/K, not really....*
04/30/2005, 4:13 p.m.

Lauren: *I can pick u up at ur hotel. Cocktail in the lobby before we go out?*
04/30/2005, 4:15 p.m.

Geneva: *Sounds great! xoxo*
04/30/2005, 4:15 p.m.

Two married women going out on a Saturday night? It was asking for trouble. Lauren tried to recall if Geneva wore her wedding ring that first day they worked in tandem. Still, Lauren knew the perfect place to take Geneva: Players, but, she was wary about going to a club without Collin's blessing. She went to find him in the living room, feet up, playing *Halo* on his Xbox 360, with a fresh beer in the drink holder of their sectional.

He leaned to the side when she approached him, so she darted in opposition, and waited for him to get shot. Die? Blown up? Whatever it was that needed to happen for him to peel his eyes away from the screen and set down the controller.

"What do you think about getting a couple guys together and going to Players with me and Geneva tonight?"

"Players? Have you been there, honey?" Collin's tone was amused, no doubt that he thought she knew nothing of the place.

Players was a brand-new club built a hop, skip, and a jump from Cassidy Gate—the main gate, at Ft. Bliss. An obvious ploy to take every last dime of a soldier's pay, it featured ladies' nights-a-plenty, sexy Latina bartenders, and a stage of stripper poles with a rickety sign stating NO PROFESSIONALS above it.

"She said she wants to go somewhere where there's a bunch of hot, drunk soldiers." Lauren replied evenly.

Collin must have been in a good mood because he didn't press for a reason as to why a married investigator would want to seek out a hot mess like that on a Saturday night. "Should I invite Angel?"

"His wife isn't going to insist on going, all pregnant, is she?"

"Naw, I'll tell him to tell her it's a guys' only thing. No wives, no girlfriends." He reached for his phone.

Lauren slid on a pair of fit and flare jeans she'd purchased when she first found out Geneva was coming down to El Paso. The black cami she pulled over her head made some allowances for her cleavage and clung to her slim waist. An inch of skin played peek-a-boo between the bottom hem of the black top and the belt loops of her dark jeans. She didn't correct it, but wisely chose a faded pink, open front cardigan to complete the outfit. It was the kind that hung long in the front and short in the back. She stylishly wrapped the extra material around her midriff, hoping it wouldn't look like she was trying to sneak out of the house hidden under a bulky sweater. At any rate, Collin was clueless when it came to fashion and probably thought the sweater was supposed to be worn like that. He even whistled as she walked up to the open garage to say goodbye. She abruptly stopped at the threshold.

Angel was in there with him, disassembling a cell phone. Collin's workbench was covered with modeling clay, a pressure cooker, a soldering iron, and a bunch of miscellaneous wires and circuits.

"Our neighbors are going to report us for engaging in terrorist activities during my re-up," she commented without stepping in all the way.

Collin wiped his hands on his jeans as he made his way around the workbench. "We'll head over to meet you guys at...what? In an hour or two? I need to clean up a little first." He grinned and pulled her over. "You look hot, sweetie, no Mrs.-super-important-investigator tonight, huh? Lemme see your hand."

She thrust her right hand up in front of his face.

He tickled her with the lightheartedness of a decent beer buzz until she extended both hands flat, palms down, out for him to inspect. She wiggled her fingers. "Never have a doubt, babe. Never." She kissed him on the lips and left for Geneva's hotel.

There was an empty martini glass lined up behind a heavily poured Cosmo in front of Geneva when Lauren spotted her at the end of the bar. On her approach, Lauren attempted to stay directly behind the tall barstool on Geneva's left in hopes of avoiding an assessment by her fellow investigator. No success. Geneva wasn't inconspicuous as she eyed Lauren's thin physique up and down. And then up again.

Weight gain was so common for women in jobs like theirs. Constantly sitting, driving, typing, stressed out...an uphill battle with no "me" time. By Lauren's second year in the field, her own clothes had begun to strain at the seams. At first, she gave in and bought all new suits. Then, during a much-needed bout of retail therapy in Lane Bryant, she lost her cool. Lauren dropped an armful of plus-sized clothes on the floor of the dressing room and bolted from the mall in tears. A quick bit of research led her across the bridge downtown to a Pharmacia for some "real" diet pills within days.

As Lauren climbed onto the barstool next to her, she considered telling Geneva how to go get them.

Geneva regarded her in shrouded contempt, masked by an overly enthusiastic simper.

It can wait, Lauren decided. She still wasn't sure if they were anything more than cyber friends yet.

The bartender wasted no time. "What can I entice you with, Cariño?"

"Same as her," Lauren quipped, wanting to waste no time with him. "How's everything going?" she directed to her friend.

Judging from the look on her face and the slump in her posture, Lauren figured she was treading on thin ice with Geneva.

"Same as DC, just desert. I got stuck out at McGregor yesterday, my tire. It got buried in the sand."

Lauren quickly took the drink from the bartender to get a gulp down so she wouldn't noticeably cringe. She'd wanted to give Geneva a folding shovel to keep in her trunk for that exact reason, but Geneva's demeanor was so off-putting that she'd scrapped the whole roadside emergency kit gift she'd prepared.

"What happened?" Lauren asked without setting down the drink. One more gulp and then she could be all ears, objectively.

"A couple of the soldiers dug me out. One was really cute." Geneva raised her glass and smiled. "I didn't realize they'd all be armed out there."

"At McGregor? Yeah, it's live fire out there, for sure. Did you hear the call to prayer?"

"Yep, if you'd have dropped me out of the sky blindfolded and asked me to guess where I was, I'd say Afghanistan, without a doubt."

"That's why they all train there before they ship out. This is the last stop, McGregor rather, before going to hell."

Geneva propped her chin up and turned to Lauren with a dazed expression. "You and your Marine, you still with him?"

"Yeah, Collin, we're going on four years."

"Well, that's a drop in the bucket, but good for you." Another gulp of the Cosmo went down with ten percent of the liquid streaming out the sides of Geneva's mouth. She wiped her face with the back of her sleeve before continuing. "Jim's fucking around on me. I filed for divorce right before I left."

Lauren's initial reaction was to resolve their divorce in the same manner she would have for a subject, but it would have been sterile and so inappropriate. Instead, she flagged down the bartender and said, "Can you bring us some waters and a menu? We're going to get a couple apps before we go."

Turned out, Geneva didn't need to be interrogated. She spilled it all. The gory details of her second husband's infidelities and the soon-to-be horrific custody battle regarding their infant son readily emerged. Lauren encouraged her to drink water and take bites of food during the showcase that triangulated self-pity, jealousy, and humiliation.

"I guess you wouldn't understand," Geneva concluded with a sideways glance to Lauren's neckline.

Lauren scanned the bar top for a salt shaker. There was none, so she laid a napkin across her plate and pushed away a half-eaten piece of quesadilla. "No marriage is perfect."

"Has Collin stepped out on you too?"

"Not with other women, but he maintains a pretty serious 'bromance' with Angel. He's prone to jealousy, err, moodiness rather. Most times I just let it go in one ear and out the other."

175

It was astonishing how seamlessly Geneva's investigator mask transformed her entire presence. "Do you mean moody regarding his emotions solely, or are there times it leads to physical encounters?"

"Are we doing my ESI now?" Lauren asked as she tilted her head to shoot Geneva a knowing look. "Or yours?"

Geneva quickly threw out a "Sorry," backed up with a giggle.

They both relaxed and Lauren explained. "When we first met, I was just a kid, without a clue. He took me under his wing, so to speak...he helped me get my shit together. He was, is, a bit older than me."

Geneva's left eyebrow arched in skepticism. "Under his wing or under his covers?"

The bartender reached for the plate between them. "All done, ladies? Want me to wrap up the rest?"

"Yes and no," Lauren responded without hesitation and turned back to Geneva in a curt motion. "I wouldn't have graduated college without him. He's always been protective of me. He gave me a safety net, you know? And now, working around soldiers all the time, he just likes to keep an eye on me, that's all. He doesn't want any of them getting the wrong idea; obviously, I am his wife after all."

"You know you sound like the poster child for a domestic abuse hotline, right?"

"That's not it, he's never laid a finger on me. I'll tell you something that might make you understand, but you can't tell anyone else. It's very personal to him."

Geneva's whole body curved toward her.

"When Collin was a kid, a demon would appear in his bedroom at night sometimes...."

"Like a ghost?"

"No, let me finish. So, according to his dad there are these things called 'djinn' and they've been intermingling with the St. Germain family since World War Two. Their leader, a red djinni called Iblis, has appeared to Collin's grandfather, dad, and then Collin himself when he was growing up in Jersey. It's called a bedroom invasion when spirits, shadow people, djinn, etcetera, appear at night to sleeping kids. Collin says this went on for a while, and when he'd yell for his parents, his mom always got irritated and brushed it off as nightmares. His dad listened though, and eventually he had to teach Collin 'coping skills' to use whenever he saw Iblis over his bed."

Geneva had the most incredulous look on her face.

Lauren paused to sip her water. "Look, I'm not saying the djinn are real or anything, but think about it: his mom didn't believe him. In a sense, she abandoned him to deal with the most horrifying thing he'd ever experienced in his life, up to that point. If that's not a justifiable reason for him to mistrust women, then I don't know what is."

Geneva held her breath as if trying to keep her opinion trapped inside.

"His dad also told him that Iblis put a curse on all St. Germain men, that they would marry women who would inevitably cheat on them." Lauren skipped the "beautiful" part of the incantation.

"And this is why he's so 'protective' of you?"

"I don't know, it's just what he says. Can you imagine growing up in a family that seriously believes they're cursed? That would skew anyone's perception as an adult."

Geneva snorted and pushed back from the bar in a huff. "Sounds to me like he's always got the perfect excuse to be a control freak."

Instead of rebutting, Lauren checked her phone. Collin had texted four times.

"Do you still want to go out?" Lauren asked, slighted. "We could call it a night."

Geneva scoffed at the idea of staying in. "Are you kidding? I'm a free woman now. And I'll be here for Cinco de Mayo next week. Let's go find ourselves some hombres!"

chapter twenty-one

Fort Bliss, Texas
JANUARY 10, 2007

In a televised broadcast, President Bush announced he would send an additional 20,000 troops to Iraq to provide security for Baghdad and Al Anbar Province. Even though the operation's working title was "The New Way Forward," it was more commonly referred to as "The Surge." Simultaneously, the war in Afghanistan increased in both complexity and intensity with the rise of the Taliban.

Two thousand seven marked the year when eighteen month-long, back-to-back deployments became the norm, and IEDs were the deadliest threat facing US armed forces on the ground. Due to its similar terrain and government-owned land mass, Fort Bliss became the training hub for most soldiers prior to deployment. McGregor Range functioned much like a FOB, engulfed within acres of the Chihuahuan desert. Training exercises were conducted several miles away from main post at a site located in a pocket of desert off Highway 54— Tobin Wells.

Collin turned off the highway and onto the gravel road leading to his shop. It was a bumpy five miles to reach the dilapidated, out-of-commission, guard gate that provided the only visual marker for the entrance to Tobin Wells. His shop was at the very end of that road, past several Patriot missile-training areas. Dated outpost structures supported a variety of obscure contractors and active duty detachments. Groups assigned to this area of Fort Bliss required ample space, primarily for Patriot Missile systems defense training.

Even though the ADA's training evolutions weren't supposed to start until February, news of the Surge caused Tobin Wells to buzz with activity. The day prior to Bush's announcement, the troops came out and set up their gear. They'd be camping out there for days— maybe weeks—to perform simulated fire missions. Collin slowed down to watch the units of soldiers deal with their array of missile, radar, and support vehicles off the side of the road. It was more crowded than usual, perhaps there were two units training this week. Temporary kitchens and portapotties were set up under camouflage mesh netting. These training evolutions were practice for the real world, live fire of a Patriot Missile. Just like Collin's IED trainings, the ADA executed every aspect of a live fire situation up to the very second the missile would be fired. Nostalgia for his eight months in that dismal Saudi sandbox kicked in by the time he reached his shop.

Had there not been any training exercises scheduled, Tobin Wells would have been a ghost town among the tumbleweeds.

Collin and Angel spent most days using their ingenuity and experience to create realistic IED scenarios for pre-deployment soldiers. Giving them a taste of what they might experience in Iraq and Afghanistan was the mission. They relied on current intelligence to keep up with the enemy. One week the IEDs in Afghanistan were cemented into curbs, the next, buried under a common path taken by US troops. Fortunately, being a little rough around the edges was an advantage. Collin's suspicious and devious tendencies proved to be an asset as he crafted IED scenes not found in standard training manuals. The more accurately he could recreate the threats in a safe environment, the better.

Their brainstorming out in the desert resulted in all kinds of storylines for soldiers to experience. They recreated a typical Afghan village, several renditions of HME labs, countless variations of IED's, and suicide vests—to name a few. Soldiers could examine all these props up close and personal, with no fear of harm.

They even had funding to hire local actors who could play the part of insurgent on training days. Since Arabic-speaking individuals were short in supply, they employed locals with the instruction to speak only Spanish. Collin and Angel both loved it when they were short-staffed on those days. Donning the traditional Middle Eastern garb, or the "man dress" as they called it, to jump in and play enemy was decided upon by who could hit a beer can with a clean shot from 300 meters. Collin usually won.

Collin turned down the radio when he pulled up to the fence outside the shop. The truck remained running as he hopped out and went for the key to the padlock. He and Angel were down to one key between them, so they kept it in a Hide a Key Lockbox stuck to the back of the sign outside the gate. Building 3716.

Collin checked the cage in the shop to inventory how many IEDES kits they had available. There were six—not enough for the updated schedule.

He dialed the number for Supply. "Hi, Amber, it's Collin over in the IED shop. How are you?"

"Hey there, Collin. How's my favorite Marine?"

He couldn't resist smiling. "Good. Can you pull some things for me to draw? We need a shit ton of stuff."

"I'll pull up my screen, just hold on a sec."

Collin debated if he should make small talk with her while her computer came on line.

When her voice returned, it was a little too animated. "Okay! What do you need?"

Someone who doesn't leave dishes in the sink overnight.

Someone who didn't continually insist that he read Autobiography of a Yogi.

Someone who might be interested in having kids....

"I'm ready whenever you are," Amber's voice cut through.

"Sorry, um, let's start with four IEDES kits, four mine kits, two cases of inert mortar rounds, and one additional case of miscellaneous inert ordinance...." Busy with planning, he fell back into neutral confidence.

Tobin Wells, the shop, hiding explosive devices in the desert—the whole environment was truly an appropriate fit for Collin.

c h a p t e r   t w e n t y - t w o

Washington, DC
SEPTEMBER 2006

Spending two days in a row with Geneva's four-year-old son was becoming too much for Lauren. By the end of the second day of sightseeing with him in tow, Lauren altogether ceased any attempt to maintain a conversation with Geneva. Her efforts to hide the mounting irritation seemed to work and she was relieved when Geneva exclaimed, "Finally, we can talk!" after dropping the boy off at his dad's.

They stopped at Whole Foods on the way home and picked up all the necessities for a proper "Girls' Night In" of dishing and drinking. With the cheese, crackers, olives, and hummus spread across Geneva's kitchen counter, the only thing left to do was open the wine. Geneva handed the bottle and corkscrew over to Lauren.

"You were a server, right? Can you open this? I'll destroy that cork."

Lauren poured two oversized glasses and opened the second one while she was at it. Both bottles were set on ice—the pajamas went on, and the feet went up, and the inevitable rant about OPM guidelines commenced. When Lauren's glass ran low, Geneva pointed back to the kitchen. "Let's just bring the bottles in here."

Lauren hopped up and fetched them along with a second helping of snacks. She laughed when she toppled to the side while sitting back down on the couch.

A moment of silence followed Lauren's outburst as Geneva's middle finger smoothly circled the rim of her wine glass. Not knowing what to say next, Lauren popped a whole cracker in her mouth.

"How are things at home?" Geneva inquired.

Lauren pointed to her mouth as she exaggerated chewing.

"Sorry, I didn't mean to ask when your mouth's full."

The chewing deliberately slowed as Lauren tried to think of an answer.

"You still with your Marine?" Geneva prompted.

Lauren nodded, swallowed, and washed it down with a large gulp of wine. "Yes," she croaked, then cleared her throat and wiped her lips with the back of her sleeve. "Of course, things are good." It came out way too quickly so she balanced it with, "There's the usual marriage stuff, but nothing out of the ordinary."

"Does he still make you wear your hair up?"

"He doesn't make me do that, he prefers it. And I don't mind, it's always hot down there anyway."

"Is he still cursed?" Geneva baited.

Lauren dismissed the question with a smooth response. "Oh, that. Perhaps, but it's more like I'm the one who's cursed, not him." It was a slippery slope, wanting to vent and save face at the same time.

Like a good investigator, Geneva didn't press the topic. Instead she emptied the wine bottle into her own glass and went to the kitchen. The clunk of the bottle hitting the bottom of the trash can caused Lauren to jump. She took another gulp—a big one. By the time Geneva returned to her spot on the couch, Lauren's tongue had loosened.

"What really pisses me off is that I was sympathetic when he told me about the shit he went through as a child." No preamble, Lauren just picked right up where they left off last year, at that hotel bar in El Paso. "It's like I'm some commodity to him. It's not just the clothes or the hair, but it's where I fall in the pecking order. He will never, *never*, say no to Angel! But God forbid I request some time alone with him, a date, or even sex— the freaky kind, too—on one of his precious Guys' Nights. Then, all of a sudden, I'm the controlling one."

"How often does he have these 'Guys' Nights?' "

Lauren shifted in her seat. "Like twice a week."

"Are you fucking kidding me?"

Lauren shook her head and drained her wineglass. "He makes me feel like I'm crazy or needy whenever I tell him that he's the one being unreasonable. The conversation always goes down the same road…that he needs to watch out for himself because of his family history. One of the lovely 'coping skills' that his dear old dad left for me to deal with."

"Does he really say that?"

"Yeah, or that I should understand, no, accept, why he can't trust women, because of his childhood trauma. His mother cheated on his dad and his grandma cheated on his grandpa. '*By all counts, I should expect you to cheat on me*,' he says…my fucking badge of honor! And I'm almost positive that his skank of an ex cheated on him while he was in the Gulf. I swear he's been on the brink of telling me that he has PTSD because of her. Such bullshit!" She lost her train of thought. "Anyway, long story longer, I'm lumped in with all of them even though I'm faithful as all get out." She laughed bitterly as tears threatened to fall. "Jesus, maybe I should. He already thinks I am. Might as well get laid out of it."

"Lauren, he has no proof," Geneva reminded her.

"There's nothing to have proof of Geneva, Jesus! But it doesn't matter, you see. I could be a nun. The St.

Germain curse officially proclaims that 'all the men with that surname are destined to marry beautiful but adulterous women.' It started at the end of World War Two when his grandfather was released from a German prison camp. When he returned to his village in France, expecting to find his wife and newborn son waiting, he found her to be on the first plane out of there with an American."

"That's awful."

"She thought he was dead. She had a baby to feed and no resources. Tragic, yes, but...." Lauren shrugged her shoulders. "So, that baby was, is, Collin's dad. He spent half his time growing up in the US with his American stepdad and *maman*, the other half of the time in France with his real father. You can imagine all the shit his real dad fed him when he was there. Thus, the origin of the St. Germain 'curse' a.k.a. unilateral ban on trusting women."

"How very convenient."

"Yeah, doesn't help that Collin's mom played around on his dad, either. Collin caught her with another man when he was a kid."

"Jesus."

The two women held eye contact for a brief instant.

"Well, you're fucked," Geneva concluded, and they both dissolved into hysterics.

Geneva pulled her laptop from the coffee table and opened it on her lap. "Maybe you need a little curse of your own to fall back on, a free pass to do whatever you want." Her smile was devilish.

"The James curse?"

"That doesn't sound quite as impressive." Geneva looked at the screen. "What was the name of those things, the genie things?"

"The djinn, um, Iblis, that's the leader of the red djinn." Lauren picked up the second bottle to refill her glass and from that point, things got a little spotty.

When she woke the next morning, Lauren's eyes felt as though they'd been glued shut. And pounded upon before the glue dried to make sure they stayed pressed together. The coffee table was directly in her line of sight from her reclined position on the couch. She didn't bother lifting her head to see (and smell) a half-full, open bag of burnt microwave popcorn next to two empty bottles of wine.

Three bottles? Jesus....

On the far side of the table sat a pint of ice cream with two spoons sticking up out of it, further cementing the warning to the state of Lauren's stomach and head. Geneva's open laptop remained on the coffee table. Lauren picked it up and slowly walked to the kitchen to find an outlet. Very slowly.

When she plugged in the device, the screen lit up on a website about the djinn.

"It is said that these entities can influence a person's thoughts and dreams simply by whispering into one's ear. It has also been said that they can aggressively enforce suggestions that eventually become actions from the person that they are oppressing."

Like a curse? No, this is all conspiracy theory bullshit. Lauren scrolled down the page.

"THE RED DJINN"

"The red entities seemingly have only one reason to exist: to bring forth the destruction and the downfall of humankind. In Islamic folklore and belief, these entities would be the closest thing to the Roman Catholic and Judeo-Christian demons. The red djinn have abandoned all previous ties to their leaders, their families, their clans, and their God, to follow *Iblis*.

"Apparently, they are very sensitive entities. They take offense very, very easily. They are known for being vindictive, and if the situation arises, they will try to get revenge against anyone who engages in any activity against them regardless of what the original intent was." [2]

The symbol on top of the blog looked like a cross made from two lowercase r's with curves connecting them at the top. It was elegant, red, and reminded Lauren of a mosque.

There were seven tabs open across the top of the screen, all djinn and curse related. Except one. Some guy named James, an actor from Great Britain *sans* shirt; it was a search done in the "images" tab on Mozilla. Lauren closed them all out and hastily cleared the browser history. She doubled over with her hands on the counter, racking her slow-moving brain for any recollection of the conversation last night.

Then she scurried to the bathroom to puke.

---

[2] LVCIFER, "Discovering the 'Demons' of Islam: A Crash Course in Understanding the Djinn, From Multiple Perspectives," *Diabolical Confusions* (blog), May 27, 2013.

chapter twenty-three

El Paso
FIVE YEARS AN INVESTIGATOR

Dani scanned Lauren's employee file from 2007 while Lauren checked her phone. They sat across from each other in a comfortable silence during Lauren's annual review. There wasn't much to discuss and both women were busy. It was the end of the DOD's fiscal year and the uptick in cases to be closed before the end of September had buried everyone.

"You came in first on the team again," Dani observed as she slid the papers across the table.

Lauren ignored them. She still had one eye on her phone. "So, that means what? I have a ten o'clock."

"I need you up at The Lab, like yesterday. Jimenez is doing double duty with all those reopens. Twenty hours of OT per week is automatically approved for anyone working on the Holmes contract right now, plus per diem, it's worth your while."

Los Alamos, commonly called "The Lab," has an official mission: *To solve national security challenges through scientific excellence.* Everything about it was classified. Anyone on the team who was assigned to conduct background investigations at The Lab was required to obtain a separate set of creds, which was issued by a classified entity. It was called the "Holmes Contract" and only a handful of Dani's investigators were cleared to work on it, Lauren being one of them. All the other investigators thought going to The Lab meant access to classified projects. Truth be told, there wasn't any super-secret-classified intrigue for investigators assigned to The Lab. It was quite boring. All the interviews were conducted in a designated meeting room off the lobby of the admin building. Lauren had been up there plenty of times and never went past that lobby. Furthermore, subjects working up there absolutely had to have their shit together. With little to no issues, all cases at The Lab were of the open and closed varietal.

Last month, Dani sent Investigator Alejandro "AJ" Herrera TDY to Big Bend who, when stopped at a Border Patrol checkpoint, had a canine sit down next to his car. Upon inspection, BP agents found a few ounces of marijuana in the side pocket of his computer bag. He made things worse when he attempted to use his creds to get out of the situation. Ironically, he was going to Big Bend for the CBP contract and not even that badge could help him. In the end, he lost his creds and his clearance. All the cases that he'd closed over the past six months had to be re-opened and re-worked, a complete pain in the ass for the rest of the team. Going back to his subjects and sources to redo everything made them all look like idiots.

Collin had called him a fucking moron the evening Lauren told him about the incident.

"Yeah, well, drugs don't always ruin a career, but drug sniffing dogs sure can," Lauren retorted.

Collin didn't even crack a smile at her joke

There's no route leading out of El Paso that doesn't have a checkpoint. None. Everyone knew that, well, except for a few celebrities. Willie Nelson, Snoop Dogg, and some other musicians had also been caught with pot at that same Sierra Blanca checkpoint. El Paso may be on the US side of the Mexican border, but getting some distance away from El Paso? Not possible without additional interior stops.

The Lab was contacted and the SO there came down hard on Dani. AJ had his Holmes creds and worked there often. Everyone on Dani's team who was cleared to work on that contract was drug tested within twenty-four hours of his arrest. Two of them failed by testing positive. By the end of that week, Dani was left with two cleared investigators for The Lab, Lauren being the senior one of them.

Now, Lauren stalled with an answer about going up there by pretending to check her calendar. She'd just purchased a class card to a new yoga studio, but she didn't want to tell Dani that.

"Is there a conflict?" Dani asked, knowing full well there wasn't.

Lauren's yen for hours spent nestled up in a dim yoga studio that smelled of incense would have to wait. "How many weeks?"

"Four."

Four always meant six. "When I get back, I only want cases at Bliss through the holidays. You'll have another investigator cleared for The Lab by then."

"Yes, she should be, but you'll need to edge up your numbers down here since you won't be in the car as much. Ten cases a week—you won't be the lead on all of them," she quickly added when Lauren's head shot up in disbelief. "That's a reasonable goal for you."

"And if I maintain those metrics?"

"I could keep you close to home even longer. I know you're sick of living out of your suitcase. I do. Tell you what, if you keep up those numbers through Q1, I'll keep you down here for Q2, maybe even Q3 if we can get one more person cleared for The Lab. Deal?"

"Ten cases per week? Over the holidays?"

"If anyone can do it—"

"See you when I get back from The Lab," Lauren cut off her boss as she grabbed her phone and left.

Six Weeks Later

It was frustrating. The first thing Collin tried to do the weekend she got back from TDY was nail down Thanksgiving plans.

It was early Monday morning on November twelfth when he started grilling her about it again.

"Can I at least get a cup of coffee before we start back on this?" she snapped. Irritation first thing Monday morning would equal a shitty week. "Please," she added with less bite. "Just give me a few minutes to look at my caseload."

Her time over the holiday weekend would primarily be spent playing catch up on reports. She didn't need to see her assigned caseload to predict that it was inevitable. There were two yoga classes scheduled in her calendar for the holiday weekend as well, but Collin didn't need to know that.

She and Collin hadn't seen each other in weeks. She knew if she didn't agree to go, it would be trouble.

Like curse trouble.

Cynicism was getting the best of her.

After all, we don't want to wake the djinn now, do we?

A cup of coffee helped to alleviate her grouchiness. She reigned in her thoughts and agreed to his plan. He'd do most of the driving, so she could just type in the car.

That would be the right thing to do.

"Thanks, honey," he said with a kiss on her cheek before heading out for the day. "We all have to make concessions sometimes."

A heavy bank of Fort Bliss cases had been assigned before she even made it back to El Paso from The Lab. She stayed home all day, working in her pajamas.

"Ten cases per week," she murmured to herself a few times. "You can do it, Lauren."

The sun was on the west side of the house when she heard Collin's truck turn into the cul-de-sac. A half-eaten bowl of cereal was still on her desk. She rushed it to the kitchen and had it in the dishwasher seconds before he entered.

"Your printer's working overtime," he remarked. When the door to her office was open, the machine could be heard all the way in the kitchen.

"Well...." She couldn't come up with anything to say about that. "Want a drink?"

"Sure."

After a quick chat over a beer with him, she zipped back to her office.

He closed the door to it when he walked by a moment later.

The stack of work grew so high that sheets of paper began to slide off the top and float to the floor. She glanced at it, but didn't get up.

No use in shoveling when it's still snowing.

Her mother-in-law, Nadine, now lived in Aliso Viejo, California. Lauren did a search for yoga studios near there and PuraYoga came up first. Seeing the professional shots of Tyler and Thom leading huge crowds in a yoga class on the beach or in some gorgeous park stunned her. She hadn't thought of them in so long. Should she surprise them over Thanksgiving? They had a La Jolla location and the schedule showed a class early Thanksgiving morning. It was being led by Thom and dubbed, "Giving thanks for a Buddha heart." The class description said it would end, not with Savasana, but with a Buddhist tradition; reciting the Five Contemplations.

How very Tyler.

The unexpected smile shrunk as her heart sank for the carefree life that she missed. They looked so happy, so healthy. How would she even begin to describe her world now to them?

The printer stopped. Time to sort, stack, and staple. She groaned and muttered, "Fuck, Dani," when an expedited case was spotted in the mix.

Case #139026871/YILMAZ
ACD: 27 NOV 2007
CD: 12 DEC 2007
AD: 20 DEC 2007

Holy Shit! Are they kidding?

It was one of seventy-six cases assigned to Lauren—all to be closed before the end of 2007.

Even though "Take out Thai" night was set to begin in fifteen minutes, she started briefing the Yilmaz case anyway, wanting to get a jumpstart on it before tomorrow. She settled in with a highlighter and got to work.

Burak Yilmaz had recently been promoted from First Lieutenant to Captain in the Army and needed his TS like, yesterday, because he'd been assigned to *Project Red One.* Lauren checked the case messages to see if there was any guidance for her about this project. She'd never heard of it, nor was there any further mention of it on the case. It was odd, having Subject's mission printed in the case papers.

She redacted *Project Red One* and faxed the altered page to Dani with a text to follow.

Lauren: *Can u do an override and re-upload page 27 to this case? 139026871/YILMAZ*
11/27/2007, 6:50 p.m.

Dani: *DONE...someone dropped the ball on that ⊗ thx*
11/27/2007, 7:01 p.m.

Lauren: *Do I need to do anything further? RE:YILMAZ*
11/27/2007, 7:02 p.m.

Dani: *Just LMK the ETA by Friday. IT CAN'T GO LATE*
11/27/2007, 7:02 p.m.

Lauren rolled her eyes and flipped over the phone before resuming the brief.

Yilmaz was a naturalized US citizen who had limited connections with his extended family from Morocco. He was nine when his parents immigrated to New York. As a child, Yilmaz was automatically granted US citizenship when his parents became naturalized US citizens. Yilmaz attended high school in the middle-class suburbs outside of New York City, graduating in the top 5 percent of his class in 2001. He joined the ROTC, left for college with the security of the Army's dime, and majored in International Business.

Upon completion of his ROTC obligations and college credits in 2005, he was stationed to the DLI where he trained for eighteen months, excelling in Farsi. His marks were high and the comments from his instructors were exemplary.

Lauren contemplated what a dichotomous nature this Yilmaz must possess. He'd be a valuable commodity for the US Army. He had the appearance of an Arab, the intelligence associated to a techie, and a certain ease portraying nuanced entitlement—a product resulting from being raised in upstate New York.

One of his recommendation letters had these comments:

...By the time 1LT Yilmaz was assigned to Fort Bliss, he'd garnered a high level of respect from his peers and subordinates. He assesses all options before coming to any decision and he has natural leadership skills. He has never shown any evidence of being conflicted due to his religious beliefs.

Lauren re-read that last sentence. It was unheard of to discuss a soldier's religious preference in a recommendation letter for a clearance. Subjects are not required to identify a religious affiliation on the SF-86, nor is it standard questioning for sources.

Her feet pushed off the desk and her chair rolled back to the bookcase. The OPM handbook was roughly the size of a phone book, like New York City's phone book, but she couldn't find any pertinent guidance on religion affiliation.

She wrote down on a Post-it, *check Mod 99 for updates—church, religious YILMAZ* and stuck it on the letter.

Collin swung his head around the door with his phone extended out toward her. "Nadine," he mouthed. Ever since his parents got divorced, he referred to her as Nadine, just to Lauren; it was still Mom to her face. He remained in the doorway.

"Hi, Mom!" Lauren hoped she didn't sound overly excited. Nadine could always sniff out bullshit when it came to her daughter-in-law.

Nadine was "*happy Lauren decided to come with Collin at the end of the month.*" That was it. She didn't have anything else to say.

Lauren neatly folded up the conversation with a "*me too*" as she wondered just exactly what Collin had been telling his mom lately.

"How much longer?" He eyed the tornado that had hit her desk.

She looked down at his phone, still in her hand, 7:20 p.m. *Fuck!* "I just have to call a subject and set up his interview, then I'll be done," she promised.

"Okay. The food should be here any minute."

"Do you need cash for a tip?"

"I got it."

Her gaze rested on the door once he left. It was a perfect example of their conversations lately. What would he do if she ran after him and unloaded a passionate kiss? Or unbuttoned his fly? The teasing thoughts left as quickly as they had come and she called the cell number listed for Yilmaz.

Yilmaz answered, and with a stroke of luck, he was available to meet Special Investigator St. Germain at his SO's office tomorrow. She needed to sight verify his US Citizenship Certificate and send in confirmation of it right away. It couldn't wait until their detailed ESI because the process of confirming the validity of a Citizenship Certificate took three weeks, minimum. And this Captain's case needed to be back to the Army by then.

She decided to go ahead and get all his lead information tomorrow, as well. The more sources she could knock out before the ESI, the better. She opened his SF-86 to the reference page. There were three stateside soldiers listed. *Perfect.*

The doorbell rang, so she shut it all down.

It was an uneventful dinner and she fell asleep midway through *The Daily Show.*

The following morning, Lauren made it to the SO's office at Third Brigade's Headquarters before Yilmaz. The intake SO was a female soldier. Lauren discreetly glanced to the center of her chest; two bars up, and then to the left: Moore. After presenting her creds, Lauren stepped back, and pulled out her phone. She wanted to make a note, a reminder to check if Moore was the Captain who uploaded Yilmaz's case into the system.

"All electronics need to be off in here, ma'am."

"Sorry." Lauren dropped it back in her purse.

Yilmaz and a Major entered and brushed right past Lauren.

"Don't worry," the Major reassured Yilmaz. "You should be adjudicated and in JPAS by January, latest, February. You'll get all the dirty little details on the whole shitstorm then." He stopped short and noticed Lauren. "Are you waiting for him?"

"Yes," she answered. Then quickly added, "Do you have a couple minutes? I could interview you for him while I'm here."

"Captain Yilmaz was just assigned to the Third Brigade. You'll have to go to his previous unit to find his people."

"How long have you known Captain Yilmaz?" She asserted a step toward the Major, not caring if she seemed pushy.

Moore's face grimaced at the sight of Lauren infiltrating the Major's space.

"Not long enough," the Major quipped and turned on his heel to leave.

Lauren rolled her eyes and turned her attention to Yilmaz. "How's it going?"

"Very well, ma'am." He produced his US Citizenship Certificate and stepped back.

Lauren sat down on the one chair provided and began copying down the details from it. It all had to be written down in longhand. She wished she could just take a damn picture of it and be off.

"It's *Project Red One*, isn't it?" Moore struck up a conversation with Yilmaz as he waited.

The twang in Moore's voice grew lusty as she gave a rather disjointed dissertation surmising her understanding of *Project Red One*. She thought it had to do with "Remote Viewing" being reinstated to assist soldiers with their efforts to locate hidden IEDs in Afghanistan. She'd also heard there was a supernatural element working with the Taliban—a demon or spook of sorts—one who could be conjured up. "I know it sounds completely cuckoo, but it does makes sense. Over there, they believe in that sort of stuff—genies, spells, dark magic—it's in their *Kor-Ran*." She gave an exasperated huff. "I'll stick to my Bible. 'Better the devil you know than the one you don't.'"

The last statement briefly grabbed Lauren's attention. Moore's misuse of the common phrase was laughable. She wondered if Yilmaz's soldiers kept this type of xenophobia on display as well. Lauren prayed that he wouldn't be dumb enough to bring up this classified project in her presence; she'd already skated around procedure by redacting the words *Project Red One* from his case file. If she'd have reported it to an SO instead of Dani, all work on the case would cease. Immediately.

And Moore would be in a heap of trouble today.

Lauren's seasoned eyes scanned the certificate once more—everything was in order.

Wait, did anything in that reference letter even specify that he was Muslim?

Moore's cough was enough diversion for the question to slip down into Lauren's unconsciousness before being reconciled. She folded the certificate back up and tapped Yilmaz on the shoulder. "Can you step outside with me for a moment?" She glanced at Moore.

Once they were standing at the edge of the parking lot, Lauren poised her pen over a fresh sheet in her notebook. "There's no one in earshot out here. Can you give me a couple leads? Do you have your phone?"

Yilmaz looked around with uncertainty.

"If you like we can go find a conference room, but this will only take five minutes."

He looked downright nervous.

Lauren had to remind herself that he was a kid and that this was his first background investigation. She'd been doing them for so long, that she'd forgotten how intimidating the process can be for newbies. "Your case is being expedited, so if you give me the names and numbers of the people you know now, I can interview them before your ESI. It will move things along, that's all."

"Am I allowed to do that?"

"Yes, here." She handed him the notebook and pen. "Can you just write them down for me?" she smoothly requested. Then she took a step back and looked off, gazing over the horizon of brown. During a glimpse his way, her eyes rested on the strained stitching of his jacket sleeve. His chest and biceps were built up in an impressive form. The too-tight jacket accentuated the V-shape created by his buff upper body. Her eyes averted away when he looked up from the notepad and she bit the inside of her cheek, certain she'd become flushed.

In the appearance of slow motion, his right arm extended toward her and the pages of her notebook flapped in the breeze. As she reached for it, she had to curl her fingers over the pesky pages to catch them in her grip. But she overshot the reach and accidently brushed back the hem of his sleeve. Her fingertips grazed his wrist long enough to be deliberate, but short enough to be swept aside as an innocent misstep. She blinked several times in hopes of breaking the hazy trance. Concerned that her face was some shade of beet, she directed her stare to his hand, and clasped the notebook into her chest.

A tattoo peeked out from the cuff around his right wrist. He smoothly pulled it down, but Lauren caught sight of it all the same.

Embarrassed by her lack of professionalism and obvious ogling, she wasted no time to get the hell out of there

---

At 11:00 p.m. on the Sunday after Thanksgiving, Lauren connected her VPN through an air card. She'd been holed up in the guest room at Nadine's for the past couple hours, typing in the last few source interviews on Yilmaz's case. She made one final sweep of the report in its entirety before transmitting it.

"Damn," she exhaled in relief, for the night, anyway. The next round of cases loomed.

chapter twenty-four

El Paso
ANGEL'S NEW YEAR'S EVE PARTY

Amber: *Happy New Year's! Btw ur shipment came in ☺ Do u want me to hold it up front?*
12/31/2007, 10:30 a.m.

Collin: *great! U2...b safe tonite and yes, will b by Wed for it. First thing.*
12/31/2007, 10:30 a.m.

Amber: *it's a big package ;-)*
12/31/2007, 12:32 p.m.

Collin: *then I'm sure u know just how to handle it ;-)*
12/31/2007, 12:33 p.m.

"Those investigators are just glorified background checkers."

Collin looked up from his phone at the new guy standing opposite of him. It was a small group of contractors hanging around the fire pit.

No one responded so he carried on with his opinion. "One came out yesterday wanting to know all about Doug's ex, if he was in arrears. I mean, he's still waiting for the fucking test to come back on the second kid. How's that gonna affect 'his ability to keep national secrets?'"

There was a general chuckle of agreement.

Collin's voice cut through. "It has more to do with if it could leave him open to blackmail."

Angel spoke up. "Collin's wife's an investigator, show some respect."

"She only works up at The Lab, though." A lie, he knew damn well that she wasn't going up there anytime soon.

"That's some serious shit," the guy backpedaled. "Sorry, man, no disrespect."

Collin shrugged and went to get another drink.

"She the one he came here with?" the guy asked.

"She's in town for the holidays," Angel covered for Collin.

The real party was taking place inside. The group of vets-turned-contractors were getting rowdy from drinking. They bonded at every turn. Every Cowboy game, going shooting at the Fort Bliss Rod and Gun Club, every BBQ...they took care of each other. They all dressed the same for every occasion, be it a party or a workday: Polo with their company's insignia on the breast, khaki 511 tactical Carhartt pants, and Timberland work boots. Collin loved those guys and they all loved their jobs, which consisted of spending their days out in the raw desert building fake bombs. Fake traps. Fake suicide vests. And catching rattlesnakes. After all, they needed something to post on Facebook that proved how badass they still were to their civilian friends.

Collin scanned the group of women crowded in the kitchen—no Lauren. No surprise there. Angel's wife thought she was stuck-up because she always cancelled last-minute. During their first few years in El Paso, Collin and Angel made plans for the four of them to go to dinner or to the movies. More often than not, Collin would get the usual text that she was caught up with work or her interviews were running long. Sometimes there was no text at all because she'd simply forgot that they'd made plans. It was a blessing in disguise, when she began traveling all the time. But now she was back in El Paso with no TDY on the horizon. Judging from her absence inside, she still had no intention of integrating with his friends.

Collin went back outside and opened his phone. A few kids scattered from the side yard at the sight of an adult.

He keyed in a text.

Collin: *What are you up to tonight?*

Delete.

Collin: *Hope you're having a great NYE*

Delete.

Collin: *Stay safe, sweetheart. Be good☺*
12/31/2007, 11:41 p.m.

Amber: *Always! What are you up to? Want to hang out?*
12/31/2007, 11:42 p.m.

He chuckled. She was so predictable.

Collin: *That wouldn't be very safe, now would it?*
12/31/2007, 11:43 p.m.

Amber: *Ha Ha;-) At Players for another hour then heading to an after-party. Here's the address. Would LOVE to hang out with my favorite Marine☺ Bring some friends....*
12/31/2007, 11:45 p.m.

He closed his phone and snuck past the fire pit to the pool. It pinged a moment later as he was trying to recall the gate code. There was an extraordinarily inappropriate, yet very saucy picture of Amber and her friend on the screen of his phone. Instinctively, Collin looked over his shoulder; no one was paying attention. He indulged in studying it for a moment before saving it to his secret porn file.

The code came back to him.

Lauren was sound asleep on a chaise lounge by the pool. She looked out of place, snuggled up in a fringed, hooded poncho, black tights, and UGGs. Her hair snaked down in a coil that rested over the front of her left shoulder. The fanned-out tail spread across the curve of her breast rose and fell with her steady breath. It had been such a long time since he'd seen her wear her hair down; he didn't realize how long it had become. No more highlights, no more layers…it was just a soft, dark brown mane framing her wan face as she slept.

Several months ago, she'd quit wearing it down in front of him out of spite when he suggested she wear it up at work. It was so sensual and she was around men—soldiers—all day. Her eyes narrowed and her lips had pressed together, but she didn't fight him on it. Instead, she wore it up all the damn time from that point forward. One night, they were about to leave for dinner and he asked, "Are you wearing your hair up in a ponytail like that tonight? For dinner?"

The look on her face dared him to continue with the topic. His mouth snapped shut and he complimented her top when they got in his truck.

Now, with the moonlight reflecting off the water, she had the look of an arctic goddess. Like the northern lights had made their way down to the southern border of the US and created beauty incarnate in the form of his sleeping wife. Collin peered down at her, all curled up in layers of fabric, and a vision of her lying on a dog sled seeped into his mind. With his eyes half-closed, he could actually see her poncho turn into a giant parka with a fur-lined hood tickling her face. No longer on a chaise lounge either, she was now reclined on a wooden, tandem dog sled, and he felt the wind pick up as the sled gained momentum. The concrete pool deck below them morphed into white snow. He could see his own boots next to her left shoulder, planted in a firm stance as the sled glided under his control.

The thought of leading a dog pack—mushing through a snowy tundra while his wife lay in contentment at his feet—it was....

There were no words to articulate it. It was just a feeling that overcame him and caused his heart to race. His breath caught in his throat and he shivered involuntarily.

If only he could turn back the clock.

In 2006, she had to take a week's worth of paid vacation or lose it. Her approved time off fell smack in the middle of September that year and she came up with this hare-brained idea to go visit Pamela on Baffin Island. It's far north, past Quebec—somewhere in the neighborhood of the Northwest Passage. There was a whole itinerary that included dog sledding and camping in igloos under picturesque views of the aurora borealis. It really had been a great idea and he should have gone. But....

Booz won a contract to put together a counter IED training program at Twenty-Nine Palms for the First Marine Division. Collin's unit was in this division when he was enlisted—C Company under the First Combat Engineer Battalion—is headquartered there. The opportunity to go TDY for the whole month of September to set up shop beckoned.

"Why can't Angel go?"

"I don't know, they said it had to be me."

Lie.

She scrapped the idea of taking the trip up north, telling him that she wasn't going to go alone. Instead she flew to DC for a week and stayed with Geneva. It left Collin feeling at odds. Geneva was a wild one, freshly divorced, but he couldn't very well tell Lauren not to go. Especially since he was the reason she was going there and not to visit her great-aunt.

His regret of not going, not taking her on that trip, had been festering under the surface ever since. But at this moment, right next to Angel's pool, he could taste the fantasy and he wanted to savor it. This vision of them on the dog sled intensified in detail as his breath slowed, allowing him to slip into a relaxed state.

A familiar growl, no louder than a whisper, beckoned. "Look up."

The camera in Collin's mind slowly zoomed out to take in the whole scene. His gaze rose from his boots up over the black snow pants, and then to his narrow waist. She hadn't stirred at his feet, even though he felt the sled accelerate beneath them. As his mind's eye continued to travel up his torso and chest, a hazy red filter tainted the image. In earnest, he made a bid to focus on his arms, which were manipulating the reins. Then his attention went past the reins to the dogs. Smoke covered them and blurred their all but faint outlines, still, they were there—running—the mountains on one side and the water on the other.

The camera zoomed out even farther, showing him the couple on the sled.

He wasn't the one driving it.

The punch in his gut felt so real that tears of rage turned to pain and stung his eyes. He rubbed them, pushing away the vision, drying away the wetness, all the while cursing and telling himself that it wasn't real.

No, there wasn't a whisper. It was my imagination.

But the desire to throw her in the pool and hold her under flashed through his head.

No! My mind is a fortress. Iblis can't breach it anymore.

Lauren's eyes opened and shot straight to his, as if she'd been awake the whole time. "Sure, he can." Her voice was melodic, almost sultry.

"What did you say?"

She yawned and stretched. "Hmm? What?"

He sat down on the lounger next to her and repeated the question. "What did you just say when you woke up?"

She looked confused and pushed up to her elbows. "I don't know. What did I say?"

"Sure...." He couldn't bring himself to say the rest out loud.

"Did you ask me something?"

He shook his head.

"Oh," she reclined back down. "I don't remember. Maybe I was dreaming." Her eyelids went heavy.

"Lauren?"

"Hmm?"

"How are you?"

Her head turned to him, but her eyes were still shut. "I'm exhausted." She sounded defeated.

"From—"

Her eyes opened as she said, "This," at the exact same time he said, "Work."

He forced himself to take her hand. "It's been a hard year."

"I wish...I just wish that...." Her sad, quiet voice was heartbreaking.

"Shhh." He put a finger over her lips. "Don't wish for anything. You can't change the past, let's just move forward."

The volume of the mariachi music roared in an invasion of the quiet space between them.

With no calculation or forethought, Collin made the next move. "I came over here because I wanted to tell you that I've been thinking. I'll go to counseling with you."

Her reaction wasn't the joyous one he'd expected.

"Why?" She sat all the way up and faced him. "Why now? What made you change your mind?"

"Ten, nine, eight, seven, six...!" the shouting from the party overtook the music.

"Um, Happy New Year, honey." His face dipped to hers.

"Happy Anniversary," she countered.

He kissed her full on the mouth.

Four Months Later

A sparsely attended *Catch 'em in CONUS* classified meeting unwittingly set a chain of events in motion that helped incubate the first homeland terrorist attack on Fort Bliss. Ironically, the meeting was held in a recently constructed, formidable building located in the newest, most secure section of Fort Bliss, known as East Bliss.

Before entering the lobby of First Armored Division's Headquarters, all electronics had to be stowed in lockers and visitors immediately reported to armed soldiers after passing through bulletproof doors. CAC card was required and one's entire social security number had to be entered on the spot in JPAS to determine the visitor's clearance level in real time.

Both Collin and Lauren had extensive access to this building, but for different reasons. Most of Collin's extended planning meetings took place there, inside one of the many impregnable conference rooms. In contrast, Lauren frequented the secure fortress to investigate those attending the top-secret meetings.

On that Thursday, the tenth of April in 2008, Collin's meeting focused on an unusual SF Group that had a brief window of time to train with him before leaving US soil. As talented as this group was, Collin's training prior to their departure was invaluable. May 10, 2008 through

May 14, 2008 were already blocked off in Collin's calendar solely for these SF soldiers. And since they were such an elite group, an advanced level of training was required. Therefore, Collin and Angel devised a four-tiered, complex scenario based on the limited information they had detailing the remote and extremely volatile mission.

Ready to give the brief, Collin thumbed through his notes on them while waiting for the rest of the attendees to arrive. This SF group was an offshoot of the Third Brigade and comprised of several unique teams. Each team consisted of the following retinue:

o   Twelve SF soldiers
o   One multi-purpose canine and handler
o   Three EOD soldiers
o   Several civilian contractors—usually two or three men to each team

Essentially, there were twenty individuals per team. With three teams, it would be a tight schedule to get sixty people through in such a short time. Plus, the dynamics within these teams were different than standard army units. The civilian contractors went down range with the soldiers, having full knowledge of the details about the classified missions.

The name of the company the contractors worked for? Classified.

Their titles? Classified.

They didn't interact with anyone except the "green suits." These mysterious contractors received constant and current intelligence about the movement of regional tribes in Afghanistan, IED activity, and Al-Qaeda operations—including all breaking Taliban developments in theater to the hour.

Collin set the papers aside when the Colonel entered and approached the head of the table. The Colonel wasted no time. "Mr. St. Germain will brief us on the field training. He has the HME lab presentation slides, etcetera."

Angel dimmed the lights and everyone but the Colonel adjusted their chairs to face the side wall screen. Projected on it was a photo of a forty-foot shipping container, a connex.

"I found this sitting one range over while Angel and I were out scouting the area around our building last year." Collin pressed a button on his remote to flip to the next image. The connex had been moved to the field behind their shop and the picture showed them transforming it into a replica Afghan residential structure. The outside had been painted a sandy color and the interior decorated with traditional Afghan furniture, rugs, and décor. Evidence of IED activity had been placed within it.

"Our experience has been that taking the troops through the connex first tends to set the tone for the rest of the training."

When Collin clicked the play button to start the short video, "Property of DoD, Fort Bliss Sub Range Ops" appeared on the screen, followed by a classified information disclosure. He entered his security code and clicked through the subsequent security measures.

The video began with Collin addressing a group of soldiers. "Tell me what you see."

Most soldiers were quick to point out the fertilizer stored in plastic bins in and around the entrance.

"Okay, correct, but that's not necessarily a problem to escalate. Many locals will have small farms and agriculture near their homes."

The camera followed the group inside. The soldiers were visibly cramped and uncomfortable.

Someone pointed out a disassembled cell phone on the side table.

Collin shook his head with a fatherly smile. "Good, but this, too, is not enough of an issue to cause friction with the homeowner. A search needs strong merit to be conducted."

A moment or so went by until they were released to go back outside. The soldiers shuffled around and began to mumble among themselves until Collin spoke over them. "Go look at the outside again."

It was just a plain container, like one on a train. A female staff sergeant raised her hand and called out, "The outside appears longer than the inside, sir."

They went back inside and Collin instructed her to lift a tapestry. It hid an opening in a fake wall Angel had erected five feet in from the true back of the connex. The camera peered through the hole to reveal a bone-chilling scene. Angel utilized the graphic experiences he endured during his most recent tour to create a mini-lab secluded in the five-by-ten-foot space, equipped with a work-bench that had a coffee grinder attached to it.

"The coffee grinder," Collin explained, "is used to reduce these small, round prills of ammonium nitrate fertilizer into a fine powder, thus increasing the surface area of the explosive medium."

The camera paused on rows of coffee cans full of rusty nails, scraps of metal, ball bearings, and other jagged things. The contents of those cans would be tightly packed inside of homemade bombs, creating shrapnel. A fifty-gallon plastic drum was pushed back into the corner.

"This drum might house the final explosive product to be buried deep below a local road or walkway." The last statement was directed to the camera in a PSA style line.

The video ended and Collin clicked to the next photo. It was a shot of the horizon from the outside of the connex. "This is what we like to call the 'petting zoo.'"

"Since the connex experience hones their focus, they tend to have more success when they trek out into the field to find our devices, our IEDs." Collin pointed out a miniscule fence hardly visible in the picture. "The farthest boundary is marked off by three rows of barbed wire out approximately 150 meters." He turned his attention back to the faces engrossed in his presentation. "We're able to immerse soldiers in realistic Afghan terrain so they can take their time to search for the trip wires, pressure plates, and so on without the fear of being blown away."

The next image was of a suicide vest. "We're still working on a scenario, but we set aside some time for this SF team to at least get their hands on it."

"Where's this being stored?" the Colonel asked.

"In our cage at the shop, sir. We've already been through the local FBI protocol with transporting it and using it for training purposes."

"Who made this?" He sounded impressed.

"I did."

Angel interjected from the back of the room. "Collin is too modest to tell you, sir, but the FBI's WMD Coordinator, Agent Jay Hart, came out to photograph the vest and some other stuff for agent training purposes. What did he say?" Angel gave Collin an appreciative look before answering his own question. "He said that Collin fabricated the most realistic IED's he'd ever seen. There was also some mention of how lucky we are to have him on our side."

"Well, I had started the prototype in my garage at home and the project grew, so I contacted Agent Hart before bringing it to the shop. Obviously, I didn't want to drive on post, or anywhere else in El Paso, with it in my car," Collin added.

A good-natured chuckle rolled through the room.

Collin went to the next slide, bypassing a tempting comment about how lucky they were to have a couple Marines working on this project. "The obvious take away here is that the only difference between our training field and theatre comes down to the explosive component. In our field, soldiers know when an IED has been triggered by a loud clap, immediately followed by a CO_2 blast that blows a non-pyrotechnic material like talcum powder everywhere. There's no missing it."

The final picture was of a couple E-4s who looked as though they'd been caught in a flurry of snow. One was smiling, the other wasn't. The shock of the blast made some of the younger soldiers laugh at first, but the humor faded as they realized its true implications.

"Thank you," the Colonel said.

Angel brought the lights back up. Collin returned to his seat and the Colonel called for a five-minute recess.

While washing his hands in the latrine, Collin's mind drifted back to last night's argument.

She was sitting in the kitchen when he arrived home, well after five. Stockinged feet up on a chair and the ceiling fan on high. The lights were off.

She pulled her reading glasses down from the top of her head to rest on the bridge of her nose and said, "Hi," as he came toward her. Her hair was in a top knot, her cheeks were flushed, and she wore no make-up, except red lipstick. There was a pencil pushed through her bun. The top three buttons of her white top were undone, showcasing some voluptuous cleavage.

She looked really fucking hot.

His cock stiffened—it was his first reaction, especially at the sight of the seductive smile that had been on hiatus for almost a year.

Something about that red lipstick, though...it caused a secondary reaction that overcame the first.

"Trying out the sexy librarian look for the soldiers today?"

Lauren's jaw dropped. The chair upon which her feet were resting? She kicked it so hard that it fell over backward. She jumped up with defiance flaring in her eyes. Her shirt was untucked and the hem was creased with damp

wrinkles. The bottom button was undone, as well. "What?"
she hissed.

"It's just," he motioned to her chest. "It's a bit much."

"It's fucking hot out, Collin. I've been in the god-
damned field all day!"

"Listen, I didn't mean it to come out like that...."

"Just because that's how you see me, right? That's
what this is, you're projecting, Collin." She threw his words
back at him as she smacked the fridge door while storming
out of the kitchen. Unexpectedly, she whirled around and
added, "Oh, my God! How very silly of me, this isn't pro-
jecting, is it? I'm just playing my part in your stupid curse,
right? The cheating wife, the slut, some soldier's whore?"

"Shut up, Lauren!"

"No! Some Marine's whore! Ever think all this," she
pulled the rest of the buttons apart and yanked her top open,
revealing a lacey black bra, "that it's all for you? There's
no one, no one else!"

The door to their bedroom slammed with the echo of a
"Goddammit!"

He reset the kitchen chair, picked up her shoes—ex-
pensive, black high heels...the kind with the red bottoms—
and chucked them in her office.

"Dude!" Angel broke in from the men's bathroom
door. "The Captain's about to start."

As he shuffled back to the briefing, Collin decided
he was going to take the rest of the day off and go buy

some new bedding for the guest room. Some sheets that didn't have pink and white lilies all over them.

"Next up is Captain Yilmaz, SME on *Project Red One*," came from the Colonel, once more in his proper spot at the head of the table.

No chairs turned or moved. Yilmaz stood at the other end of the table—the second head—in equal footing with the Colonel. "Mr. St. Germain, your slide show was very impressive. I look forward to going through the training with the troops next month."

Heads bobbed up and down in agreement.

The peanut gallery.

"I'll keep this brief, much of the information we're working with is considered to be hocus-pocus, scoffed at by Western military strategists, usually likened to fortune tellers and such. Nobody goes on record, but there's a very real concern that there truly are otherworldly entities at play in the Middle East. That is the basis of *Project Red One*."

The fact that no one in the room seemed surprised by this would cause most to pause and reevaluate their belief systems.

"The death toll from IED attacks in the past three months—compared to the first quarter of 2007—suggest that the number of IED-related casualties will triple in 2008. We expect this to be the deadliest year in Afghanistan to date. There's a clear correlation between the claims made by a growing, mystical sect of the Taliban, and the number of deadly hits from their IEDs. They claim to be consulting forces in the other dimensions, the non-physical world. The information gathered through this divination, if you will, provides them with the best co-ordinates to bury IEDs as to make the most lethal impact on our soldiers. At these locations, IEDs are positioned in scenarios that draw the troops into a trap by giving them a false sense of confidence. A dud IED will be found by one of our scouts, maybe a second one not far from the first. Seeing no threat, the troops waiting behind the scout will proceed. It's a ploy, the bulk of the live, um, I mean working, devices are placed just after the two duds. This puts the group at risk, not just the individual scout."

Some heads, including Collin's, had dropped down to blankly stare at the packets set out by Yilmaz during the break.

"This could be written off as new tactics, but it's the origin of the idea to draw in the troops that's disturbing. The enemy is setting up these scenarios only at coordinates that fall directly in the line of our troop movement in Afghanistan. Accurate coordinates. Extensive investigation has ruled out double agents on our side. We believe the source behind their knowledge of our paths comes from where they say it does. Deal making with the djinn." Yilmaz took a pause and adjusted the cuffs of his jacket.

Most of the heads popped back up, but not Collin's. It remained down in a signal that he was completely engrossed with the papers clasped in his hands. An almost imperceptible gasp initiated a choking feeling in his throat.

"Since tribal populations in the area already have a deep-rooted belief in djinn involvement with daily life, they have pledged their support to this mystical sect, which is now growing exponentially in power and status within the Taliban hierarchy."

Collin barely heard what Yilmaz said next as he tried to piece together the information being presented. The underpinnings of this classified project hit home. Very close to home.

Coping skill number six came to mind.

Repeat this, son. Repeat it until it is part of you.

"My mind is a fortress. I maintain control of my thoughts. Nothing can breech my fortress," Collin whispered under his breath so quietly that no one glanced his way.

After letting the words sink in to his psyche, Collin's face lifted to watch Yilmaz for the remainder of the presentation, still only half listening. His father's mantra repeated on a loop in his head. By the end of the briefing, it had sunk in and he was secure. Confident, even. Destiny had brought him to his life's mission: training US Army SF troops how to detect and defeat Iblis.

chapter twenty-five

El Paso
MAY 10, 2008

"I told you, Angel's son's birthday party was tonight and you said it was in your calendar. Natalia thinks you're snubbing her. Again. What am I supposed to tell them now?"

"That we had these plans for months."

It was Saturday morning. They were five minutes early for their weekly marriage counseling session and still sitting in Collin's truck, splitting hairs about who told who first. Lauren was certain that she'd asked him to attend a yoga workshop taking place at White Sands that night. It was a partnering class designed to create new, energetic pathways between couples. After, there was to be a drumming circle under the stars, and the option to camp overnight. She'd signed up and paid for them both to go in February.

"Months?" His tone was so patronizing that she wanted to slap him.

Practicing her own coping skills, she clenched her thighs together in a Muhla Bandha lock so she wouldn't strike him. Her voice gave her away, though, as it trembled with rage. "All I'd be doing is sitting on a friggin' patio chair next to Abuela, while you and Angel are off in his garage. You said you'd come with me, in like, February."

"I know it's hard for you to understand, Lauren, but kids...well, their birthdays are really important."

"Go then, I wouldn't want to interfere with your loyalty." She swung open the car door and didn't wait for him to walk in with her.

The counselor, Louise, had her work cut out for her today.

Once settled into the counselor's designated "safe space for a peaceful exchange," Lauren wasted no time to speak first.

"This yoga workshop is really important to me, it's a partnering one, and he agreed to go, but now, Miguel's birthday party trumps our plans." She only paused to come up for air. Her emotions were amped up from the moment she stepped into the room and she felt claustrophobic. The La-Z-Boy chair that was supposed to be relaxing squeezed her from all sides and her bra felt more like a compression tank top. She felt trapped in her marriage and it manifested in her physical body, almost choking her at every turn.

"Who's Miguel?" Louise asked evenly.

"Angel's son," Collin responded.

"Five-year-old son," Lauren emphasized.

He shot his wife a scathing look.

It was a waste of twenty minutes, going 'round and 'round on the same unresolvable topic. Collin put his social life with Angel over Lauren. She was sick of discussing it and cut off Louise with, "He's gonna go to the party and I'm gonna go to White Sands tonight, that's it. Do we have to drag this out?" Lauren squirmed in her seat.

"Excuse me," Louise emphasized as if to remind Lauren of her manners. "Take a breath, Lauren. Remember, resolution needs to come from a place of calm." She wrote something in her notebook. "Now, may I continue?"

Lauren's fingertips dug into the armrests of the slate colored La-Z-Boy as she forced herself to sit back.

"Collin," Louise started in a friendlier tone, "last time you expressed a concern about your wife's choice of yoga instructors. Is it possible that you're making," she glanced at her notes, "Khulu a scapegoat? Perhaps her yoga class represents something else to you? You had mentioned how you wanted her to connect with your friends."

"No, my concern has to do with him. His class is basically a harem. She just doesn't want to admit that her guru's more interested in copping a feel than spiritual enlightenment."

"Oh, my God, Collin, really?" Lauren rolled her eyes.

Louise held up her hand. "Let him express his concerns, it's his turn."

"I went to a class with her, like we agreed." Collin looked to Louise like they were on the same side, warranting a smile from the counselor. "And this Khulu guy was all over her, like it was some sort of Kama Sutra class. He singles her out. Is it so wrong that I don't want my wife being fondled by some curry-eating pervert?!"

"Tell her how you feel," Louse encouraged.

Collin squared off his shoulders as he looked to his wife. "I don't want you going there anymore. Find a female teacher, unless you prefer to have some stranger's hands all over you."

"Jesus, don't I get to say anything to this?"

Louise held up both hands. "Collin, find a less aggressive way to express your feelings. Lauren, be open to what he's trying to tell you."

"I'm just trying to protect you. I don't think you understand how men...."

Louise's rules had gone out the window for Lauren. "Protect me? From what? What, exactly, are you trying to say, Collin?"

Now they both ignored Louise's raised hands.

"What do you think he imagines when you show up wearing those skimpy tops? What do you think any man thinks of? You're running around all over Bliss in your fuck-me shoes with your tits on show. It's like you're begging for the starring role in every soldier's spank bank!"

Everything went red. "I've been nothing but faithful to you! That curse...I'm not your mom, I'm not that whore you were obsessed with! Just because you see me as...like that...like a piece of ass doesn't mean the rest of the world does!" Lauren jumped to her feet, causing Louise to shrink back and Collin to sit up straighter. "You think I don't know why you played Daddy with me? You think I'm a fucking idiot, Collin? Not everyone is as fucked up as you are in the head. And that curse...."

He shot to his feet and grabbed her arm.

She pulled out of his grip. "That stupid, fucking curse! If you keep treating me this way, it'll be a self-fulfilling prophesy."

There was only four feet between them, largely taken up by a coffee table littered with blue and aquamarine glass décor. Those items were supposed to represent water and be calming. But there were so many that the table top looked cluttered. Collin shuffled around the corner of the table, grabbing at Lauren, and the knick-knacks trembled. Oblivious to the counselor, Lauren scrambled and tripped into her. Louise broke her fall and both women crashed on top of the table, sending a wave of blue everywhere. Louise hopped to her feet and backed away. It was only a matter of seconds for Lauren to get to her feet as well and she confronted her stunned husband head-on.

Lauren's open palm flung across his face with a crack. He reacted by grabbing her shoulders and shaking so hard that bruises immediately formed under his fingers. Since the table took up so much room, neither of them could become grounded or balanced enough to land a solid blow.

Louise couldn't get between them, so she began shouting, "Stop! Stop it!"

Lauren's head rattled as he released her with a shove back down into the La-Z-Boy. She was like a cat drenched in water, arms and legs flailing. He made a start for the door, but her foot shot out and kicked him. She missed the center target of his groin, but only by an inch.

"Motherfucker!" He doubled over with his hands covering his crotch. "Fucking bitch!"

"Mr. and Mrs. St. Germain!" Louise screeched. "Collin! Sit down!"

There was no choice for him to do anything but fall back into the couch while he gasped for air.

"Stay down, Lauren," the counselor ordered. "Violence is never…it shouldn't ever have to come to this."

Lauren reached down to pick up one of the upended glass sculptures.

"Leave it," Louise instructed.

"We'll pay to replace the broken ones, I'm so—"

"I'll add it to your bill," Louise cut her off. "Procedure says I should call the authorities."

Collin's head perked up and Lauren's hand went to her eyes.

"I'm aware of the ramifications that would have on you both." She took an especially hard look at Lauren. "I'm not going to involve law enforcement, if I feel confident that there can be a twenty-four-hour cooling down period between you two. Lauren, you go home, and Collin, you'll have to spend the night elsewhere.

Lauren glanced sideways to see him briefly nod in agreement. It's what the police would have done if this had been a domestic at their residence.

"Twenty-four hours," Louise sternly warned, "minimum."

"Go ahead and take my truck. Angel will come get me." Collin slid the keys across the table.

"You leave first, Lauren," Louise advised.

Lauren snatched the keys and beelined for the door. Her emotions were spinning out of control and she couldn't think straight; getting out of that room was all that mattered. The drive home was foggy, punctuated by tiny gulps of air every so often when she remembered to breathe. By the time she pulled up to the driveway, she'd decided to skip the yoga retreat. Her emotions were divided; she had a little crush on Khulu, but it wasn't worth her marriage.

Her hands rested on the steering wheel after she cut the engine in the garage. "Fuck him," she tried, but there was only regret and resignation behind the expletive. Her head hurt and her heart was broken. Accepting defeat, her forehead sunk to the top of the steering wheel.

Her nose wrinkled. The ashtray was partway open and the stale smell of stubbed out cigarettes made her gag. With a sigh, she pulled it out and went to dump it in the trash can. White filters with lipstick poked out from Collin's tan ones.

"Fuck him!" She left it, still full, on the trash can lid. He'd figure it out.

After a shower and a Xanax, coupled with a glass of wine, she poked around in the pile of things she had collected over the past couple days for the yoga retreat. Sleeping bag and egg crate for the bed of the truck, pillows, a stocked cooler, yoga mat, emergency kit....

"I would never, never, let that lid fall down on your fingers."

She loaded it all up in his truck, except for an over-sized fleece and a pair of sweatpants; those went back to the bedroom. There was a black Lulu halter hidden in the bottom of her dresser drawers with the tags still attached. After smoothing it down on her body, she started for the closet. She did a double-take in the full-length mirror. The neckline was a deep V and the built-in bra did wonders for her cleavage. It had been a long time since she'd seen herself in such a sexy top...she'd forgotten. A pair of hip-hugging, black, low-rise yoga pants were neatly folded on a hanger, concealed under a suit jacket. Once dressed, she brushed her hair and reached for a ponytail holder. She paused, and slid the hair tie over her wrist. She stepped into a pair of platform flip flops embellished with rhinestones on her way out the door.

There were three messages on her phone when she checked it on Highway 54 heading toward White Sands. The last carried an URGENT notification.

chapter twenty-six

Monday Night
MAY 12, 2008

"I want a divorce."

The papers were on the kitchen table between them.

chapter twenty-seven

El Paso
MAY 13, 2008

Collin's patience and focus had been put to the test all day. His concentration on the AAR repeatedly crumbled until the countdown to log off due to inactivity blinked on his screen. The shop was a mess at 4:00 p.m. after dismissing the soldiers from the VBS 2 classroom, where they'd been in front of computer terminals all afternoon preparing for the following day's field training. A dress rehearsal, without the expenditure of fuel or calories.

"Bro, where are we putting the extra munitions kits?" Angel called out from the cage as he struggled to carry the heavy crate of inert weapons.

"What?"

"The munitions, there isn't room for all of them in the cage. I could just stow them down under your desk. We'll be back here first thing in the morning anyway."

The computer screen locked, before he saved the last draft.

"Yeah, whatever...."

Once the crate was out of sight, Angel dropped down on the stool next to Collin. He opened his mouth to say something, but was interrupted when Collin's phone pinged.

Amber: *Sorry to bug you, but any chance u can give me a lift to p/u my car? at Lube-xpress? Greg left for day.*
05/13/2008, 4:23 p.m.

"Been working that?" Angel grinned.

"What?" Collin peered down at the phone. "No, just a ride here and there. It's always something with her damn car."

"Maybe you should."

Collin snorted in agreement? Disgust? His intention was indeterminable, even to him. "Maybe...."

Collin: *Sure.*
05/13/2008, 4:25 p.m.

Amber: *Do u have some time to talk?*
05/13/2008, 4:25 p.m.

Collin tilted the screen toward Angel.

"You sure do. I'll finish up here."

Collin surveyed the shop once more. At least two hours of clean up still needed to be done. "I'll set up tomorrow," he offered.

"Consigues algunos panochota." Angel clapped him on the back and went back to the cage.

Collin: *Sure*
05/13/2008, 4:27 p.m.

Amber described her Saturday night with such detail that he could visualize the outfit she wore, the aftermath of the drinks she consumed, and how her skirt rose when she worked the pole to the delight of a group of PFCs egging her on from the bar.

"Will you go in with me and make sure they're not ripping me off?" she asked Collin when they pulled into the parking lot. Her flirtatious banter lightened his mood.

"Yeah, of course." Collin made a show of protective masculinity when questioning the mechanic. There really weren't any extraneous charges on her bill, but he got the guy to take off the air filter they'd installed.

"All I'd have to do is go down the block to Auto-Zone and put it in myself."

Amber beamed.

He walked her over to the car, keys in hand, and opened the driver's side door.

"Collin, I don't know if I should tell you this," she began.

His hand remained on the door and he leaned in to put the other one on the doorframe, enclosing her. "Well, then don't." His voice was low and his breath warmed her cheek. "I don't need any more drama." He got a glimpse of her floral bra when she shifted to put her lips in alignment with his. He stifled a moan and kissed her, a confident kiss with pressure that left no room for misinterpretation.

Her hands went to his neck, on his shoulders, and then her palms slid down his pecs matching his pressure.

He deserved this, especially after everything he'd been through this past year. Besides, no one had to find out, so no one would get hurt.

She pulled back first, panting, and the crown of her head drove into his chest. "Collin," she said, her voice muffled, "we should really talk before this goes any further."

"Lauren and I are getting divorced." His hand went to Amber's loose hair.

"Why?" She resisted the traction from his hands, attempting to bring her lips back up to his.

Since her resistance was unwavering, he took a small step back. "Gotta smoke in there?" he managed to ask without sounding desperate.

She pulled out two menthols and handed him the lighter. He lit one and moved it from his lips to hers. Encouraged that they puckered and lingered at his fingertips, his hand lazily caressed her cheek before lighting his own. From a distance, they merely looked like two people taking a smoke break.

"I'm too controlling, too selfish, too suspicious, too jealous—I don't mean to be. We've been going to marriage counseling." He cringed at that and took a long drag. "I don't trust her, there's something about her...." He stopped short of referring to the curse. Telling Amber that his wife was destined to cheat on him because of the boogie man would send the young girl packing. "You've met her," he broke off. Reiterating how attractive his wife is would also lead to blue balls. "I just don't trust her, plain and simple; I trust my instincts. So even though she swears up and down that she's never cheated on me, I know it in my gut that she's lying."

"Do you have any proof?"

He shrugged and took a drag.

"Without any concrete evidence, she'd end up getting a huge portion of your pension or disability, if you have either of those...." Her voice trailed off, waiting for some confirmation of her assumptions. When there was no response, she asked, "You know that, right?"

Another shrug.

"Don't you care? It was your service that earned you…." She looked to him again before concluding. "Whatever it is you may have. Why should she get it?"

"Gut feelings don't stand up in divorce court."

"What if I could give you the proof you'd need?" Amber flipped the butt of her cigarette away.

His arched through the air after hers.

Her hand rested on his forearm in a practiced manner of one used to giving others bad news. Or shitty advice. "I saw her Saturday night at Players, Collin, honest to God. That's what I wanted to talk to you about."

"She went to some yoga thing at White Sands, you probably saw someone who looked like her."

"No, your truck was there. That's the only reason I didn't drive right past the parking lot. It was her. She was sitting up at the bar with another man."

Not even a hint of friendly flirtation remained in his eyes as tunnel vision encompassed his line of sight. "Tell me exactly what you saw."

She retrieved the phone from her purse and gave it to him with the pictures already pulled up on the screen. "Isn't this her?"

Sure enough, it was. Lauren sitting at the Players bar with a dark-haired man. His back was to the camera, but his muscled arms showed that he was neither white, nor black. Indian…Khulu? It had to be that yoga teacher.

Regardless, Collin plainly saw that this guy was thinner than Khulu and had shorter hair.

"You can swipe through the pictures."

What he saw hit him harder in the groin than her kick from Saturday morning. That counseling session, it was forever ago; everything had changed now. Vindicated, yes, but there was no sense of satisfaction, like he expected.

He finally reached the picture that captured the man's face. It wasn't Khulu or some unknown hippie Indian guru type she liked, but Captain Yilmaz. Lauren, his Lauren, on the barstool next to him, her body curved toward him, with a smile flashing his way. The Captain's posture was relaxed as he took a swig of beer and had a look-see of her cleavage.

Was she wearing a push-up bra under that top? Jesus!

Another couple swipes and he reached the shot that sealed her fate. Amber must have followed them from a few paces back to get the one of him holding the door open for Lauren. The last one was of Captain Yilmaz, looking over his shoulder while following her out.

"They left together. I'm sorry." Amber sounded sincere.

A monotonous computer voice buzzed in his head: *Does not compute, does not compute.*

"Um, I didn't follow them outside. But when I left, your truck was gone." Her voice sounded faraway.

Does not compute, does not compute.

"Do you know him?"

"No." A lie that snapped him out of his trance.

"Another smoke?"

"I need you to text me those pictures. I need them, uh, I'm sorry, Amber, really. I…I have to go." He backed away with a stumble.

How?!

When?!

Where?!

With no capability of forming a complete sentence to say good night to Amber, he sped off to the shop. Not a single intelligible thought came into his head either. The drive there was just a blur of desert pierced by a red horizon.

Once there, he sat in his truck with the engine running for several minutes until Angel emerged from inside. Collin cut the engine and put in a dip.

"What's up?" Angel tentatively approached the vehicle.

"Let's take a walk." They headed out a familiar trail past the training field, toward the general direction of McGregor Range.

"How do you think she recognized Lauren?" Angel asked once Collin finished talking.

"She ran into us over at the Burger King off Cassidy Gate about a month ago."

"I bet that went over like a hooker in church," Angel joked, a weak attempt to get Collin to crack half a smile.

"Right." Collin sat down on a railroad tie and spit out the remaining dip. "That Captain was fucking here today. *Today*, man. That motherfucker!"

"Yeah, yeah, I know. We should've put him in the man dress. He seemed kind of nervous, but shit, it's hard to tell why. I mean, who wouldn't be in that group? He's barely a Captain. Unless…do you think he knows you're her husband?" Angel's tone was cautious, as it should be, this situation was explosive and put everyone at risk. Any action taken by Collin would likely backfire and land them both in the center of a bureaucratic mess with Booz and the Army. It wouldn't even matter if Lauren really was sleeping with some Captain or not, Booz's security department wouldn't want anything to do with the scandal and Collin would be out of a job. Possibly a clearance, too. "Does he have a beef with you?"

Collin looked away and exhaled. "That *Project Red One* he's the SME on, does it mess with your head?"

"Naw, the government loves its pet projects. We just do our job—detect and defeat, brother." Angel waited as Collin appeared to be debating what to say next.

"That Captain doesn't know me from Adam. Maybe she sought him out, maybe they just met by chance. Fuck if I know."

"Did she come out here over the past few days?" Persistence for a logical explanation as to why Collin's wife and Captain Yilmaz would have been together Friday night couldn't be ignored in Angel's tone.

"No."

"Maybe she's interviewed him? Source? Subject?" Angel's game of *Twenty Questions* was starting to become annoying.

"It's a huge fucking security breach, you realize that, don't you?" Persistent nudging combined with the invisible voice that had been whispering in his ear since he left Amber won. Collin's train of thought doubled down and blew past the station at full speed.

Angel put his hand on Collin's shoulder, causing an unexpected jerk. "I know, but sleep on it," he said slowly and released the firm hold on his friend. "You can vent a little, maybe even write up the report, but save it as a draft. Don't send it. Once you get the SO involved— opening that can of worms—there's no closing it. We'll keep an eye on the Captain tomorrow. You'll need those pictures from Amber, too, and make sure to tell her to delete 'em once she sends 'em. They're all you got keeping you from a lifetime of alimony, but no one'll care if they came from your little something-on-the-side."

Back at the shop, Collin assured Angel he'd finish cleaning up. "I need a 'cooling down' period before I go home, anyways," he parroted the marriage counselor. "She's usually asleep by nine. I'll wait 'til then."

"Good idea." Angel paused at the door. "Amber text you those pictures?"

"No, not yet."

Once alone in the shop and on the computer, the blank security disclosure template beckoned, and the temptation to take her ass down squashed all reasonable thought.

He typed it out and saved it as a draft. He found himself unable to press the "submit" key, so he called the hotline instead.

"A married federal investigator is having an affair with an active duty officer who's the lead SME on *Project Red One*. Her badge number is 6599."

chapter twenty-eight

Collin lay in bed wide awake as the wind whipped through the shade sails out back. The intermittent banging of the side gate clapped several times in a row. Inevitably, it would stop at the exact moment it became too annoying to bear. Not allowing any relief or silence, it would start up again.

He'd been up most of the night thinking, replaying the conversation he had with the female SO from Booz. The whole thing escalated when he finally disclosed that the investigator he was reporting was indeed his own wife. As he admitted it out loud, he knew he should have slept on it, like Angel had suggested.

The SO talked him off the ledge and advised him to hold off on submitting the draft, which would automatically open up an investigation in the system.

"*At this point, you've only called in for guidance,*" she'd emphasized.

The information he provided was merely noted within the Booz security department. She documented his statement and told him that she'd file it away—just a blip on the screen. However, if any further issue-related incidents regarding Investigator Lauren St. Germain or Captain Burak Yilmaz came about, then a full-fledged investigation would be instigated. The SO also informed Collin that he had the right to send in his report at any time. Or—and she stressed the *or* part of her statement—he could simply delete the draft. She ended their phone conversation with the same advice Angel had given him.

"*Sleep on it, Collin. Give it a few days, at least.*"

Later that night, he tossed and turned in the guest bedroom until 2:00 a.m. The small bed was too soft, so he crept back into their bed. He took care to restrict the extension of his extremities as to not creep over the invisible boundary in the middle. With a scant few hours of sleep, the hangover from the nightmare he'd been existing in for the past few days roared in full force throughout his body.

"Did you lock the gate last night?" Lauren murmured, even though her back was to him.

"Got it," he muttered. He went outside to put a brick at the base of the gate. The forceful gusts had blown over all the patio chairs, too. He took his time to stack them back up, wanting to avoid any conversation with her. All he needed to do was get through today's training without speaking to anyone about what happened last night and then he could delete the draft. A smattering of dust whipped against his calf, causing him to lift his other foot and use the edge of his flip flop to scratch it. Today was going to be a long, dirty day from hell.

"It's nasty out there," he reported as he closed the slider.

She made a hiccup of a protest from the bed without moving.

His first instinct was to tell her to be safe. She'd be driving most of the day and haboobs brought visibility way down.

Fuck her.

Collin kept one eye on his phone as he headed to the kitchen to make coffee. There wasn't anything in the fridge for breakfast, as usual. Lauren never caught onto the idea of keeping a stocked fridge.

Collin: *Heading in early, f'n haboob☹, burritos and mexi-coke?*
05/14/2008, 5:30 a.m.

Angel: *Think the roach coach will be out in this shit?*
05/14/2008, 5:31 a.m.

Collin: *Yes.*
05/14/2008, 5:31 a.m.

Angel: *Alrighty then, my brother. Bring it.*
05/14/2008, 5:32 a.m.

His battery was at 62 percent and when he went to plug in his phone, he tripped over her yoga mat rolled up on the bedroom floor. He started to kick it out of the way, but some grit caught his attention. He unrolled it with his free hand and shook a mass of white sand from it onto the tops of his feet.

No movement from the bed.

chapter twenty-nine

The Morning of the Attack
4:56 a.m.
MAY 14, 2008

In defiance, Lauren pretended to be asleep as the gate banged over and over. He came in late last night, so he was the one who had left it open.

When Collin finally got up to stop the banging, she imagined what it would be like to wake up without anyone else around. Everything would be silent if she chose not to get up right away. Or she could play loud music when she showered. Maybe she'd get an espresso maker—unless there was some kind of coffee maker that brews for one—she wouldn't need a whole pot.

When he shook out her yoga mat on the shag carpet, she had to bite her tongue from yelling at him. The white, silt-like sand was a pain in the ass to extract. Her eyes squeezed shut as she heard him drop it back on the floor. When the bathroom door closed, she sat up and glared at it. She'd heard his phone chiming earlier, so she reached to his nightstand. It was just Angel. Burritos for breakfast...*gross.*

With the water running from behind the bathroom door, she scrolled through his contacts. Whenever a new female showed up in them, she'd conduct her own little "investigation" on the name. So far, they were all work or VA related. Some of them she knew, most she didn't, but there was one that gave Lauren a sinking feeling in the pit of her stomach.

Amber.

During one of their counselor-mandated lunch dates, Lauren met Collin at the Burger King off Cassidy Gate. It wasn't especially romantic, but convenient. That's when she put a face to the name.

Lauren could tell the girl knew Collin immediately, just by the way her eyes lit up when she saw him. He stuttered over a couple words when he introduced them. Amber—from Supply—was young with a wild air about her. She even reminded Lauren of herself not so many years back.

Occasionally, a text would pop up on his phone from her. Lauren had never read the entire thread between them before. A glance down at his phone displayed the beginning of it, usually something like: *What time are u picking up the...or...We're not open Friday, put in ur order early....*

But this morning, any respect she had for his privacy had exited the building. She'd convinced herself that he dumped the sand from her mat on the carpet as some kind of message. Some sort of "Fuck you" statement that she'd have to clean up after he left.

One more pass through his texts and no Amber. Lauren even started a text to her from his phone, looking for a past thread to populate.

Nothing.

Lauren feigned sleep while Collin finished getting ready. Confronting him with an erased text thread wouldn't solve anything. When the truck engine faded to silence, she rose to get a cup of coffee. The divorce papers were neatly folded up on the counter next to her mug.

Let's talk about what happened Saturday before we make such a big decision. I'm not ready to give up on you...or us. I love you.

A glimmer from the stars she had in her eyes so long ago briefly shone into her heart as her fingertips rubbed the slip of paper.

We.... Us....

Before getting dressed for work, she crawled back into bed—on his side. Her nose burrowed into his pillow and, with his sheets wrapped around her, she wept for a few moments. The comfort of his scent surrounding her brought a calm stillness. There was still a chance for them.

She blankly stared at his nightstand before rallying to get up. His alarm clock came into focus. She smiled. He still had that same one after all these years.

She was almost fully dressed when she saw his CAC card. Doing something nice—something helpful—could be the perfect peace offering. He wouldn't be able to log in to his work computer without it. She snatched it up and tucked the ID in her purse. There was enough time to stop by the shop before her first appointment of the day.

Her phone pinged as she pulled out of the driveway. With both hands on the wheel, she merely glanced down to her phone on the center console to catch a glimpse of the text header.

Collin: *Please, honey....*

She didn't open the phone or read the entire message. Whatever needed to be said between them could be said in person. And it could wait another fifteen minutes or so.

Twenty-One Minutes Later

As Lauren slammed the car door, she instinctually picked up the pace and burst into the shop a little feistier than usual. Collin wasn't in there, just Angel, who told her that he was out back, in the training field. She flew out with a rushed, "Okay," over her shoulder before stumbling in the parking lot. She stopped short at the edge, though. If she strode toward him, her high heels would get eaten up by the rocks and goat heads.

"Collin!" Her hoarse voice was drowned out by the howl of the wind.

He stood and turned. He was too far out in the field to hear her, so she just opened her arms and shrugged her shoulders, hoping he'd understand.

Okay, let's give it a try.

She made out the smile that appeared on his face as he chuckled and a small sob of relief escaped her mouth. She imagined them running toward each other to meet in a passionate, heartfelt embrace, like lovers who've been separated for a long time do in the movies.

He took a step in her direction.

She started to slide her heel out of her shoe. She'd run barefoot.

But something caught his eye....

That's when the blast slammed her teeth together and shocked her ribcage in the oddest way, causing her to think she'd just been hit, like a giant gong. At the exact same time, a smattering of shrapnel blew into her, ripping holes into her suit and burrowing into her flesh. One of her eardrums burst and rang loudly.

A plume of smoke rolled in from the center of the petting zoo all the way to Lauren at the edge of the parking lot. It was suffocating and she began to cough. Her eyes burned and watered as she tried to make out Collin's form in the distance. "Collin!" she hoarsely yelled. "I'm over here! Are you okay?! Collin? Oh, thank God! Are you okay?"

He emerged from the smoke as a floating outline that came to a stand hovering over her. Everything about the way he was moving—especially his silence—confused and frightened her. When he bent down to pick her up, she screamed in terror.

The figure wasn't Collin, not her Collin. It was a disturbing replica with charred skin peeling from its face. He...IT—whatever the figure was—growled at her, neither human nor animal in sound. Her functioning ear heard the demonic noise, and at that moment she knew what this figure was: Collin's childhood nightmare had come into fruition before her eyes.

"Iblis," she gasped, that was ITs name.

The red djinni loomed inches above her face and gloated.

"I command the angels to protect me from your evil!" Something inside her clicked and the sum of all her substance garnered authority. She knew that angels were the only beings capable of overpowering the djinn. After all, she'd always paid close attention to Collin's ghost stories. They had been imprinted upon her.

There was an incandescent burn for an instant as red fury flashed. Iblis swooped in, as if to devour her. ITs claws grabbed hold of her shoulders, accurately targeting the bruises still visible from Collin's own rage. As IT shook her, she used every ounce of strength—physical and spiritual—to claw at the ground.

Collin's boot appeared on the ground next to Iblis.

This is all a hallucination, her mind rationalized.

Collin was coming to save her. It was his steel toe Timberland and it wasn't burnt. In fact, it was cruelly intact, still holding his left foot. As well as what remained of his charred, bloody leg—right up to the knee joint. That's where it had been ripped from his body and projected toward her as a blood offering. Her black high-heel lay just a foot or so past it, also burnt to a crisp. By now, she was very much aware that this was not a hallucination, and that she had been screaming the entire time.

The blast had exorcised this demon from Collin and now Iblis was coming for her, his next of kin.

It was all true.

Rough hands grabbed under her arms and tried to pull her away, but Iblis seemed to have a hold on her.

Angel struggled with her writhing body. "Goddammit, Lauren, don't fight me! This could just be an initial blast. We've got to get back. I'm the only one who can get you out of here."

Angel won in the tug of war for her body, but Iblis made a final strike. She howled at the blow to her groin—an inch from the center, to be exact. It knocked the wind out of her.

Angel hooked his elbows under her armpits and dragged her away from the blast. Her legs dangled like a rag doll, painting a trail of blood on the gravel. Once he had her on the pavement of the parking lot, he repositioned his hold and picked her up like she was a child. She went limp and her head dropped to his shoulder. He took her into the shop and set her on a workbench. It was difficult to determine the severity of her injuries.

"Stay still," he ordered. Angel grabbed at the first aid kit, causing QuikClot bandages and tourniquets to tumble all over the floor. He ripped open a couple of the combat bandages and thrust them to her.

"911, please state your emergency."

"There's been an explosion at Fort Bliss, Building 3716. We're out at Tobin Wells. There may still be active explosives out here." Angel helped Lauren press the bandages on her side with the most visible bleeding.

Metal scraps were poking out from her left torso and blood was running down her legs. "I have a badly injured civilian female on site and there is a male whose whereabouts are unknown. Get the EMTs out here now!"

"I'm dispatching El Paso Fire as we speak. Are you injured?"

"I don't hear the sirens. Where are they?"

"They're en route. Please stay on the phone with me, sir. Are there any others at your location?"

They appeared to be alone in the shop at first sweep. He shot over into the cage. "She and I are inside the shop, it's a large warehouse-type building. We're friendlies. I don't know what's going on outside." He switched sides with the phone so it was between his left ear and shoulder. "Stay with me, Lauren, c'mon, girl."

Lauren was the only one who saw the blast, but she still couldn't discern what happened out there. It was like a live IED had been detonated, but that was impossible. They never used real explosives.

"Sir, are there any armed people at the site? Fire is less than three minutes from your location."

Silence.

"Sir?"

"I don't know. I can't see the field, there's dust from the explosion and the haboob. Damnit to hell, I wish I had my weapon. I hear the sirens."

Within minutes a fire truck arrived. Then the ambulance. Then the local PD. The MP right on their heels. None of the authorities approached the shop, though, so Angel scooped her up and hustled out the back door to meet them.

The wall of guns drawn didn't faze him. "She needs help and I fucking work here."

By this point a team of Army EODs arrived to take the lead. They moved swiftly to create an inner perimeter around the shop and an outer boundary that blocked off a gigantic portion of Tobin Wells with orange barricades.

An unarmed EMT cautiously crossed the line of drawn weapons in his approach to their targets: Angel and Lauren. Any threatening behavior made by Angel would result in all three of them getting mowed down with bullets. The EMT gingerly tried to pry her off Angel.

Unaware of the imminent need to not make any sudden movements, she clung to him, screaming, "Get Collin, Angel! Why aren't you going back for him? Iblis is out there! Collin needs your help! It was Iblis!"

Angel's attention snapped to her. "Did you just say it was Yilmaz? Captain Yilmaz?!"

"Tell her to let go of you," the EMT demanded as he jockeyed around them with a needle poised.

It was a pressure cooker. Bandages were half-hanging from her skin. Her erratic movement and Angel's attempts to subdue her were making the police visibly anxious. On top of that, everyone was trying to remain vigilant. They could have been surrounded by devices rigged to explode at any moment.

Or not.

The EOD sergeant, decked out in desert camo tactical gear and khaki, hard-knuckled gloves, unloaded the first of several Talons without blinking. He hailed to the lead police officer. "Stand down! He's supposed to be here! There's at least one casualty in the field!"

Reluctantly, the weapons lowered, allowing Angel to manhandle Lauren and help the EMT hold her down on the gurney so an injection could be administered. The EOD sergeant strode over as she clung to Angel's hand. Then a second EMT stepped in with handcuffs.

"Give her another shot," Angel ordered.

The two EMT's looked at each other. "This one's taking effect, give it a moment."

The EOD sergeant and Angel huddled over her. She caught bits and pieces of Angel's voice as he briefed the sergeant on their objective. Her death grip on his hand began to loosen just as he started in on some specific details about Collin's devices.

"All his bombs look realistic," she slurred, "only some of them go off."

They ignored her, or pretended to ignore her, she couldn't tell as she closed her eyes and listened.

"They're gonna be the most realistic-looking IEDs you'll ever encounter," Angel advised and then hesitated. He looked down at Lauren before continuing with a tight voice. "There may be a second individual in the field, a Captain. He's brown, Middle-Eastern brown, not sure if he's on our side, though."

The only information that was known for sure was for the past month, Collin poured his extensive knowledge into crafting six different IED scenarios for highly trained SF troops to find at this location. At this point it was assumed that, somehow, all of his devices had become live overnight. EOD had their work cut out for them.

The sergeant's face remained impassive even though Angel had just dumped a mountain of convoluted information on him. Most people would have high-tailed it out of there, ASAP.

"Collin is her husband?" the sergeant asked, glancing to Lauren.

"Yes."

"And for sure he is…?"

"Yes. Out there." Angel motioned to the field behind the shop.

"And she was…?"

"In the parking lot, calling to him."

"What was she doing here?"

The EMT interrupted them. "Can we go now?"

"Let me get a Talon out there and do an initial sweep first. Is she stable enough for now?"

Lauren's eyes were glazed, but she was still awake. Her body hurt. It hurt down there. Fortunately, the drugs they'd shot into her made it possible to compartmentalize her pain.

"For a little bit. Beaumont's not too far."

She rolled her head to the side to get a better view of the scene. The EOD sergeant released the first Talon. It bumpily rolled to the edge of the field with its camera transmitting real time imagery back to a screen in their van. A line of black Chevy Tahoe's swooped in on the scene, all identified with GS plates. A cloud of dust formed when they skidded to stop in a linear formation behind EPPD.

She recognized WMD FBI Agent James Hart as he exited the lead Tahoe and rushed over to her and Angel. Hart was the one who came to their house the day Collin finished the suicide vest. He was always making stuff like that in their garage.

Maybe Iblis was influencing him to blow up our marriage....

"I'm sorry for your loss," Hart spoke slowly in a loud voice over Lauren.

"Back off," Angel muttered under his breath.

A shuffling occurred. Light was blocked, then open, blocked, then released. The two men carried on with a discussion, standing over her gurney. She couldn't make out everything, but Angel repeated the name Yilmaz again.

No, she told him it was Iblis out there, right?

Angel must not have heard her correctly. What would that Captain, uh, Yilmaz have anything to do with this anyway? He wasn't SF. Angel wouldn't know him.

An image of Yilmaz wearing a crisp, white shirt breezed through her head. He was handsome that night at the bar. She had tried not to stare when they spoke.

"You need to go with them." Hart said sharply.

Angel leaned down to speak into Lauren's ear. "If your boy, Captain Yilmaz, had anything to do with this, they'll hang you, too." He released her arm. Light flooded her sight.

The last thing she saw was one of Hart's cronies making a show of pressing Angel's head down. He guided Angel into the back of a Tahoe like he was being booked.

c h a p t e r　t h i r t y

Two Days after the Attack
MAY 16, 2008

"Lauren, you need to keep your eyes open." There was a female soldier sitting next to her hospital bed at WBAMC. Lauren struggled to make out the rank symbols on her uniform, but she couldn't lift her head high enough.

Several hours passed before Lauren could stay up and carry on a conversation that lasted longer than five minutes with this Major Catherine Miller.

Miller explained that she'd been assigned to be the primary psychological provider to Lauren St. Germain. "All they've told me so far is that you witnessed the blast out at Tobin Wells. It sent the entire post into lockdown."

Lauren's eyes dropped to the manila file on Miller's lap. Even in her current state, she recognized a case file when she saw one. "Does the Privacy Act of 1974 apply to me right now?" Her voice was raspy as she spoke her first words since the breathing tube had been removed.

"What do you want to know?"

"Transparency." Her eyes succumbed to closing and she dozed off for a few seconds. "What are you looking at on me?" she mumbled a moment later.

Miller thumbed through the case material. "Well, we pulled your employment history, your most recent background investigation, your security file, JPAS, NSA, DHS, TSA, you know the drill."

"A deep dive?" Lauren's eyes fluttered open. Pulling information from all those extra agencies indicated that Miller was at the start of a criminal investigation, not a background investigation.

Miller's "mm-hmm" was barely detected.

I need to remember this, Lauren thought and she fell back down the rabbit hole.

Two hours passed.

The next time her eyes opened, they were overrun with images of Fort Bliss. Miller must have turned on the TV. The news displayed the aftermath from the event she'd personally witnessed at Collin's shop. Images from the "Fort Bliss Attack" had been running nonstop on the cable news channels.

Fort Bliss enacting FPCOM Level D stirred up banal emotions of what it might be like to live under a police state. Fort Bliss is a massive military installation and functions much like an independent city. Tire spike strips were popped up at every gate. MPs toting ballistic shields herded soldiers and civilians alike back indoors with all the propagation of martial law.

The rolling headlines under the images repeated that Wednesday morning's events in the outlying Tobin Wells area were not accidental. Thousands of individuals had been detained on post for up to twenty-four hours in conference rooms and auditoriums. The explosion had officially been labeled as an act of terrorism, domestic or foreign was still unknown, but a "homeland terrorist attack" nonetheless.

Lauren couldn't keep her eyes open as the words *Booz Allen Hamilton contractor* started the next headline. Her head bobbed down. The nightmare she had been living took a breather as she dreamt of manila folders and innocent victims.

Over the course of her career, Lauren systematically saved logs with thousands of case names and numbers listed in chronological order. She kept those cheat sheets under lock and key in her home office. The last time she'd gone through them was when a CBP officer used his standard-issue gun to kill his cheating spouse. His background had been done by someone on her team and only three of them possessed CBP creds.

She rushed home that day in a panic and scoured the list for SMITH/CBP041034598. She'd never forget how light-headed she felt when she slumped in relief on the floor next to her safe. It wasn't hers, it was AJ's.

When he returned from administrative leave, she met him for a drink and he told her everything about his trial. CBP denied liability, claiming OPM had granted a TS to an unfit individual. OPM denied liability by claiming its own adjudicator didn't follow standard guidelines. The adjudicator blamed the investigator, claiming that key information had been missed, or worse, ignored, in the field.

Smith's family was compensated with a settlement and AJ returned to work—shaken. Seeing the images of the deceased female, shot in her own home, it changed him.

"You have to make peace with this," Lauren had told him. *"You did everything by the book."*

She buried the initial reaction of guilt that flashed in AJ's eyes when she had said that. That dead wife was speaking to her now, during this patchy dream. Lauren tried to hear what she was saying, but it was just out of earshot. She strained to the victim's face, but an old, weathered, Spanish-style wooden door had closed over the woman.

The sound of a door's automatic locking mechanism clanked and a figure entered the hospital room. Maybe it had just been the nurse all that time, walking in and out of Lauren's hospital room.

All OPM case material received from field investigators was indefinitely housed in an underground storage facility beneath the Iron Mountains in Boyers, PA. It's hard to nail down the exact size of it, but saying it was like an underground football stadium was close enough. Investigators were not permitted to keep or destroy their own case material. Everything had to be turned in, even a scrap of paper with a phone number. There was no expectation for an investigator to recall anything about cases they'd closed. Their notes, case materials, and papers could be accessed if any questions about a subject surfaced.

With all these regulations in place, Lauren was confused by the name being spoken over her bed.

Bald One: "Iblisilmazzzz, you have to recall Subjectttt."

Her head looped around. There was that damn manila folder again.

Miller: "Lauren, you need to keep your eyes open."

Her whole body still hurt like it was on fire.

"Tell her to open her eyes again."

"Lauren?"

There were three people in her room now and sunlight streamed in from the window. Miller stood next to a couple men in suits. Lauren was beginning to realize they were in the middle of a conversation.

With her.

"Who?" Lauren asked them. She knew that she was starting to come to because she wondered just how many times she'd said "Who?" right before that moment.

Like an owl.

"Burak Yilmaz, a Captain, you completed his background investigation and saw him four nights prior to the explosion. In a non-professional setting," the bald one responded.

Lauren looked from one man to the other. She assumed they were IA, from the internal investigations department of OPM. She couldn't recall when they entered the room or if they presented their creds.

Furthermore, she couldn't possibly imagine why they were asking her about that fucking Yilmaz case and not telling her what happened out at the shop. "Where's Angel?"

"You were the lead on the case, in fact you interviewed almost all his sources, even the ones out of your territory. That's odd, isn't it? That you would do phone interviews for a TS?"

Lauren shifted to find a comfortable position. Someone had adjusted her hospital bed while she was sleeping and she was now upright. It was excruciating. She regarded the three officials for a tense moment. Something was wrong. "I don't understand. What does Captain Yilmaz have to do with this?"

The appalled looks she received from all three of them was an omen. A horrific omen.

"You met him at a bar...?" The bald one was condescending with this statement/question, like he was asking her if she had been a bad girl after she'd been caught.

"It was a subject re-contact. I can't control where he said to meet me." Her tone grew snappy.

"Where did you two go together after the bar?"

She shook her head in shock. This was really, really wrong.

Lauren looked to Miller. "Where's my OPM liaison?"

No one answered.

"What blew up in the field?"

None of the officials standing over her bed made any move to answer or comfort her.

Lauren looked around the room. "Why isn't there a phone in here?" The quick movement of her head caused such searing pain that she gasped and involuntarily clamped down on the button to administer Fentanyl into her IV. But, before the drug hit, she saw what she was looking for—two armed MPs outside her door—the kind that aren't stationed in the hall to keep people from getting in. They were there to keep her from getting out.

Miller advised that everything was fine when one of them stuck his head in at Lauren's yelp. Once the self-locking door sealed shut behind him, Miller tapped Lauren's hand.

No response.

Bald One: "Let's talk in the hall."

Miller: "This is the only room not under surveillance, defendant's rights."

Bald One: "Mrs. St. Germain!"

No response.

Stay awake, stay awake...you need to remember this.

"Dani Bragg has been in the lobby raising hell all morning. I can't put her off any longer without jeopardizing our position here." Miller. "I have to preserve this woman's mental and emotional health. That's my oath as a practitioner. Now, go back to your higher-ups and get the right sanctions in place. Then you can come back and question her properly. I'll make sure she's stable, but we have to cross our t's and dot our i's now."

The trio left.

Lauren's limp hand lifted to smack her own face. It felt like a brush on the cheek, so she went for her side with gumption. Her eyes involuntarily popped open—that did it. She wiggled around to get a glimpse of the unobstructed view from her fifth-floor window. The parking lot was below. What she saw sent fear pulsing through her body. It tethered to the pain.

A zoo of press vans, newscasters, and crowds were all shoved up against the barricades on the far end of the lot. The crowd looked like it would breach the barriers at any moment in a riot.

WBAMC was front and center in the unfolding news of a homeland terrorist attack.

The headlining story on the national stage?

"A survivor from the massive IED attack at Fort Bliss is being treated for wounds at the Beaumont Army Medical Center near Fort Bliss. It has been confirmed that Special Investigator Lauren St. Germain is not only the primary witness to this attack, but that she is one of the architects of this horrific event unfolding in El Paso, Texas." The blonde anchor's face was replaced with an official photo of Lauren St. Germain, the same one from her creds.

It was a shitty picture of her, too.

chapter thirty-one

Washington, DC

"The claim that you were having an affair with Yilmaz won't be addressed in there," Lauren's lawyer stated with relief just seconds after checking her Blackberry. "And they still won't reveal the protected source who made the report about you two with Booz. They probably fabricated the whole thing—fucking red herring."

Lauren winced.

"How's your side?"

"Fine. Does that mean they're not even going to ask me about it?"

"If you had an affair with Yilmaz? No. They're going to have you retrace your steps from the time you left your house Saturday night until you came home the next day. Every breath, look, word you shared with Yilmaz needs to be addressed. It should corroborate with your movements tracked from your SIM card. Thank your lucky stars you had your work phone with you that night."

"If I hadn't, we wouldn't even be talking about this." Lauren inhaled deeply before emitting a long, slow exhale to calm her nerves. "What about the pictures? Don't I get a chance to defend them?"

"All those pictures do is prove everything you're testifying to, there's nothing to defend."

Lauren cast an uncensored *are-you-fucking-kidding-me?* look in her lawyer's direction.

"Okay, okay…seriously…do you need it fucking spelled out again? Since there's no evidence that you were having an affair with Yilmaz, there's no reason for you to be asked about it during the trial. And you will not bring it up either. You have no statement about this vile rumor, nor does the DOD. End of discussion, you understand that, Lauren?" It was a rhetorical question and the lawyer continued in a softer tone. "There's nothing you can do about the pictures being released to the public. Anything that's reported on them is hearsay, so don't worry about it."

It sounded so harmless when the lawyer put it that way, but those photos damned her to a guilty conviction across the US. She was the cheating whore who had an affair with the Taliban's first ever known double-agent,

Captain Burak Yilmaz. She rigged his background investigation so he'd be cleared for a TS. Allegedly. This allowed him to train for a classified mission with SF troops. It gave him access to her husband's IED lane. His sleeper cell could then target a training exercise that brought the highest number of SF troops together in a secure location. In the middle of the night prior to the attack, Yilmaz and his cell replaced the pyro charges with explosives in all the devices. Except the first two in the petting zoo, after all, the troops and their entourage needed to congregate deep in the field for maximum casualties. If there were a few straggles standing at the edge of the parking lot near the field, they'd only be injured.

Like Lauren.

When it came out that Lauren filed for divorce the Monday before the attack, it was all over for her. That *breaking news* shot to the top of the list for Fox's talking points.

The DOD, OPM, and DOA refused to comment on the pictures. But, a source (who had close, professional ties to Collin St. Germain) was quoted as saying: *"Their heads were tilted into each other when they were talking at the bar and she was smiling the whole time. Captain Yilmaz paid the tab and then he left with Special Investigator St. Germain."*

Lauren fought the urge to swallow something stronger than Ibuprofen as she shifted on the bench. Even though her body was raw and on fire, she didn't want anything clouding her head during her testimony. They'd be coming, any moment now, to bring her up to the stand.

"How much money do you think that girl, that Amber, made from selling those pictures?"

The bailiff swung open the double doors before the lawyer could answer. "Break's over, they're ready for you."

They walked in shoulder to shoulder and sat down on the defendant's side. The lawyer slid a piece of paper on the desk for Lauren to see: *Your focus needs to be in here, not out there.*

"State your name."

"Lauren Madeline St. Germain."

"Do you solemnly swear that you will tell the truth, the whole truth, and nothing but the truth, so help you God under pains and penalties of perjury?"

"I do."

"You may be seated."

The courtroom was packed and everyone who was required to wear a uniform donned the most impressive, most decorated, ware of their branch. All eyes were focused on her and she kept hers to the ones she knew—

her lawyer and Dani. Dani had already given her testimony and sat in the front row. Lauren flicked a look her way and then rested a hard stare on the prosecutor.

She was bluffing with a practiced act. Truth was, she'd never felt more alone in her life. The months of PT, that was the easy fight. Round two—the trial—began before the ink was dry on her *release from medical care* papers.

"When did you first become aware of Yilmaz?"

"I was assigned his case on November 12, 2007 and had in-person contact with him that same day. His case was an expedited case that was required to be closed by me no later than Tuesday, November 27, 2007. It was a tight turnaround, but his case was fairly standard by OPM's standards."

"A fairly standard case? What wasn't *completely* standard about it?"

"He was a naturalized US citizen from Morocco. This was the first time I'd ever come across an applicant who was naturalized from somewhere other than Mexico or the Philippines. I had to sight verify his naturalization documents on the twelfth, when the case was assigned. I met him at his SO's office to inspect them. We usually don't sight verify those in the field for OPM cases, just CBP, Customs and Border Patrol."

"Was there anything else that was unusual about his case?"

"I reviewed my extensive notes many times prior to this trial; his paperwork and case fell within the same norms as other Officers of his rank and age. There weren't any D issues, that would be D as in Delta, the most serious degree of offense ranked on an A, B, C, D scale. He had issue 11, foreign contacts, obviously, but I resolved those issues completely and in compliance with the OPM handbook, not only with him, but with all sources."

"Sources are references who provide testimony to Subject's character and loyalty to the US."

"Correct."

"Out of seven sources you interviewed on Yilmaz's behalf, four interviews were conducted over the phone and only three in person."

"Yes."

"OPM allows a limit of two telephone interviews per case."

"Generally speaking."

"No, as a rule."

Lauren took a deep breath before she gave the only defense she really had. "OPM allows exceptions to this rule which include:

1.   Soldiers who've had multiple duty stations and deployment in the past five years of service.

2.   There are no C or D issues on the case.

3.   If the case is being expedited by DOD.

4. Lastly, if the investigator obtains approval by the TL…Team Lead.

All four of these factors were present on this case."

Dani nodded slightly at Lauren.

"Your TL confirmed the same criteria had been met." The prosecutor glanced down at his notes.

"Is a response to that required?"

He smiled wolfishly as he approached the stand. "No."

Lauren folded her hands in her lap.

"What time did you leave your residence in El Paso on the night of May 10, 2008?"

"6:48 p.m."

"Can the record show that she left at 18:48?"

The judge turned to Lauren. "Please refer to all dates and times in the military format."

"I apologize, I left my residence at 18:48," she said staring only at the judge. Then she turned back to the prosecutor.

"Tell the court what happened from that time until the following morning."

Lauren wished she had worn something different that night.

"There were three texts on my work phone. I checked them while I was heading north on 54. They were from my boss, Dani Bragg. A case I had closed in November of 2007 had been reopened by the customer,

OPM, because an unusual financial transaction was discovered in Subject's bank records. There was a cash withdrawal from Subject's account in the amount of $80,000 that could not be sourced. That means they couldn't determine where the money came from when it hit his personal checking account. Whenever anyone withdraws $5,000 in cash, the bank requires a form to be filled out, usually by hand, stating the reason for the large withdrawal. Subject's written reason was deemed illegible during a bank audit and that triggered an investigation into his account. OPM was also notified—standard procedure— and they pulled his case. There wasn't any information regarding this withdrawal in his case papers, nor was any information about it developed over the course of his background investigation. So, per standard procedures, they sent the development back out to the lead investigator in the field—me, in this case—who is responsible for making contact with Subject for issue resolution regarding the matter. It's called a subject re-contact."

"Why couldn't his 're-contact' wait until Monday?"

"Dani's texts indicated that he was about to deploy and his clearance needed to be solid before he left. We call circumstances like that *Catch 'em in CONUS* cases. It's imperative to make contact with Subject while he is in the Contiguous United States. Time is of the essence."

"Did you know that he was deploying with the SF troops training with your husband, Collin St. Germain?"

"No. I was unaware of his MOS."

"Describe the 're-contact.'"

The way the prosecutor made air quotes every time he said "re-contact" was really fucking annoying.

"Since I was away from my computer, I called Dani and asked her to look at the case in PIPs. I pulled off the highway, jotted down the pertinent information, and then called Subject to see if I could come to his location."

"You had his number?"

"His phone number was visible on Dani's computer screen while she was on the phone with me. I asked her for it during our conversation while I was on the road."

"And then?"

"I called his cell phone number. He said he was at Players and that I could come there to meet him. We meet subjects and sources at a variety of places in the field, so I determined it was acceptable to go there, resolve the issue with him, and then leave."

"It seems unprofessional—"

Lauren cut him off with, "I've conducted six-hour-long interviews, sitting on an overturned bucket under a two-by-three net at Kamal Jabour, while a live fire training evolution was taking place. We go where we need to go."

"Understood. What happened when you arrived at Players?"

"I located him at the bar and sat down. I explained to him that information had been developed over the course of his investigation that needed to be discussed. Per OPM guidelines, I gave him the opportunity to disclose a suspicious cash withdrawal by asking him all the OPM handbook required questions regarding this topic. He indicated a negative response to the questions, so I confronted him with the withdrawal."

"Confronted him? Verbally? With documents?"

"There were no documents. I said, 'Can you please explain an $80,000 cash withdrawal from your personal checking account on Thursday, November 8, 2007?' He laughed and made a joking 'whew' sound."

"Did he seem nervous?"

"No."

"Then what?"

"He explained that his parents transferred $50,000 into his account on the first of November in 2007 and shortly after (he didn't recall the date), he pulled $30,000 out of a Roth IRA he had and deposited that into his personal account, as well. On the eighth, he withdrew it all in one lump sum so he could pay cash for a brand new 2008 Ford F-350 on Friday the ninth of November. Then I ran down all the standard questions pertaining to financial matters. All his responses were negative, meaning no further issues were developed."

"Did you have a drink at the bar?"

"I had a glass of water. He asked me if I wanted a drink when I sat down. Initially I declined, but after a few moments, I flagged down the bartender and asked her for a glass of water. I did not want him to order me a drink, even water."

"But he paid the tab…."

"He paid his tab, yes. I left a dollar on the bar for the bartender. They don't charge for water."

"Then you left together?"

"We exited the building together. I needed to sight verify the VIN number on his truck for the report."

"The photos show him holding the door open for you as you exited."

Lauren's lawyer interjected, "Object."

"I'll put it another way. Do you confirm that he held the door open for you when you exited the bar?"

"He did."

"Were you impaired or intoxicated? Making it impossible for you to open the door for yourself?"

"No."

"Why did he open it for you then?"

"Your Honor!" Lauren's lawyer jumped to her feet. "Witness cannot be expected to know why Yilmaz opened a door."

"Overruled. Enough with the door, counselor. Soldiers open doors for civilian females, end of discussion."

The prosecutor looked back to Lauren, whose face remained still as stone. "Did you get in the car with Yilmaz?"

"Yilmaz had a truck, not a car. He unlocked it, opened the driver's door, and then moved a few feet away so he was standing next to the headlight. I stepped up onto the railing. I had to lean between the open door and the cab to see the VIN number from the outside of the windshield. I had a small flashlight that I held between my teeth. I needed light to see the number. I copied down the number while balanced on the rail, checked it for accuracy twice, and then climbed down. I thanked him for his time and left."

"Why didn't you just stand next to the hood and copy the number from that vantage point?"

"The truck had a six-inch lift kit on it."

Snickering from the gallery echoed throughout the courtroom.

"Order!" The judge banged his gavel once.

"Did Yilmaz tell you that?"

Lauren looked to her lawyer in exasperation, but she didn't object.

"No, I...you can just tell when a six-inch lift's been put on a truck."

"When did you transmit the report, documenting all this information?"

"Sunday afternoon when I got home from an overnight yoga retreat at White Sands."

She braced herself to give a play-by-play of every minute from leaving Players to Wednesday morning, but the prosecutor walked back to his desk. He dramatically turned back to face her at the last second before sitting down.

"Just one more thing, Mrs.? Or Ms.? Which do you prefer? Ms. St. Germain, is that okay?"

Motherfucker.

"Didn't $80,000 seem like a lot of money for just one truck?"

"I wouldn't know."

"You didn't check it out on the internet? *Kelly Blue Book*, perhaps?"

"That's out of my scope as an investigator. An adjudicator would make that determination. My job is to objectively present the information given to me by Subject. It would be inappropriate for me to further investigate and assume why he paid what he paid. It's referred to as a 'separation of spheres' which keeps an investigator from stacking things to be in any subject's favor or disfavor on a case.

"Still, wouldn't you bother to take the time for a quick search Monday morning just to see if this price is accurate, if his story made sense?"

"No."

"That's understandable, I suppose, you were probably too busy filing your divorce papers downtown." He sat down with a shit-eating grin as Lauren's attorney hopped up. "Retracted, your Honor. The prosecution rests."

Lauren stayed in a safe house for two more weeks while the menacing "they" figured out what to do with her. Eventually, an exoneration was determined to be appropriate since she could be viewed as the grieving widow to a national hero who was sacrificed so that almost one hundred valuable troops were not destroyed in the live field that day.

Her lawyer flew back to El Paso with her to help for a few weeks. And to deal with the press that had been camped out in front of her house.

chapter thirty-two

El Paso
DECEMBER 17, 2008

Lauren sharply looked up from her tablet where she'd saved an MLS listing for a secluded condo in Malibu. The headline finally broke to the AP.

Her lawyer peeked through the blinds. "They're just about to burst through that barricade. Turn up the volume, Lauren."

"All allegations against Lauren St. Germain, widow to Marine Corps Combat Veteran and 9/11 hero Collin St. Germain, have been dropped. As you'll recall, he was the Booz Allen-Hamilton contractor who was tragically killed during the Fort Bliss IED Attack led by the first known Taliban Operative, Burak Yilmaz. Yilmaz was a former US Army Captain, born abroad in Morocco and naturalized to become a US citizen in 1992. Special Investigator Lauren St. Germain was accused of aiding Yilmaz by concealing critical information during his background

investigation, which she conducted in November of 2007, six months prior to the attack. Ms. St. Germain has been exonerated of these charges. We'll take a closer look at the investigation leading up to this decision, as well as a look back at the horrific events surrounding the Fort Bliss IED Attack during a special 2-hour edition of Newsbreak with Anna Mayes. Her guest tonight is Amber Pierce-Smith."

"Why don't you go out there and do some damage control about Ms. Pierce-Smith's allegations?" Lauren questioned with a cocked eyebrow. "You can beat her to the punch."

"You knew an official statement about her, or her photos, would never be part of the deal."

Lauren tilted her head back and sighed. "*Andale pues.*" She went to her bedroom and locked the door.

chapter thirty-three

Fort Bliss National Cemetery
JANUARY 1, 2009

"Are you ready, ma'am?" The soldier looked at the widow through the rearview mirror. His eyes didn't hide the fact that he was disgusted she would bring some faggot with her to visit her dead husband's grave. Before she could respond, he rolled down his window and flashed his CAC card to get past the heavily guarded gate.

Usually, only one soldier is assigned to the lone gate at Fort Bliss National Cemetery. That soldier might spend his day without incident, just blindly checking the IDs of loved ones entering to visit their fallen heroes. Sometimes a student photographer wanders in to capture the pebble expanse that contrasts the jagged mountains. The rows of indistinguishable gravesites create stark images, perfect for balanced photos.

But today it had been swept for bombs and closed so that the notorious Lauren St. Germain could finally make the pilgrimage to her husband's gravesite, since she had been held under federal charges for causing his death at the time of his highly-publicized funeral.

His mother received his flag.

Lauren sat motionless in the back seat, while Tyler checked his phone one last time before silencing it and tucking it away in his jacket. He'd pulled out the stops with an understated, but exquisitely cut suit, sewn up especially for him. He was a throwback of glamor all the way down to the *Aveda* pomade, perfectly slicking his hair back to accentuate his refined European features. The oily smell of lavender was starting to make her eyes water, so Lauren cracked her window.

"Lauren! Lauren St. Germain! Is it true Yilmaz's suicide note professed his undying love to you?"

"What was the deal you cut with the DOD?"

"When was the last time you had contact with Angel Rodriguez-Torres? Lauren! Lauren...just one more...."

She quickly shut the window and Tyler awkwardly patted her forearm. He was not one for displays of physical affection, but he really had no idea what to do. And she was so unresponsive, so dull.

"I hope you only took half a Xanax, or whatever those hordes of pills scattered on your bathroom counter are. You need to be surefooted when we step out of this car," he whispered in her ear while his eyes remained glued on the paparazzi swarming the car

The gate opened to a long road leading to the dead. It had a median down the center of it dotted with billowing American flags. They stood regally above the well-maintained grass, the only strip of vegetation in the otherwise tan gravel pit.

The car rolled to a stop at the end of the road and the soldier put it in park. "I can drop you here and let you go in on your own, or I can escort you."

"We'll go on our own," Lauren responded with surprising clarity.

The soldier kept the car running and crossed his arms in a show of insubordination. He would be damned if he was going to get out and open the door for that slut.

Tyler pulled a condescending face to the E-4 before reverently walking around the back of the car to open her door and offer his hand. She ignored the soldier and stepped up to Tyler, the only person in the world who showed up to visit Collin's grave with her.

Once they were out of the car, Tyler remarked, "I don't know how you put up with that."

"I don't. I don't even hear it anymore." It was a dreamy, far-off statement.

There wasn't a cloud in the sky and the wind had settled to a light breeze. Lauren knew where to go, but she got caught up in a stupor as she stood in front of a large plaque at the entrance. She was looking right at it, but not truly seeing it. Or comprehending it.

The quote etched in the stone on it read: *If I owned both Hell and Texas, I would rent out Texas and live in Hell.*

She cocked her head to one side, thinking she must have misread it.

"What does that say?" Lauren asked as Tyler peered over her shoulder.

His thin eyes squinted. "It says you need to get the hell out of Texas as soon as we're done today."

In a momentary lapse of relief from his dry humor, a half-titter exhaled from her nose. But, that small breath didn't crack the wall of grief cemented around her.

Tyler's face instantly turned somber and he formally took her arm. There was a quiet pageantry about the way he walked her out to Collin's gravesite. All the onlookers, cameras, and protesters were sequestered far back from the property as Tyler kept her in a bubble. His air indicated that the act of merely escorting her to pay her respects was in and of itself a religious devotion.

Lauren hurt all over, in every way imaginable, but she didn't want to cry, not here. A blood vessel had burst in her right eye from the constant sobbing she'd indulged in for weeks. Oversized sunglasses hid the bright red crackle to keep the gawking at bay. She was raw.

As they trekked along, the only noise was the faint crackle of the bandages that were taped all over her torso. They brushed against her blouse with each step and their edges were rubbing against her tender skin. The combination of all of it made her want to scream.

But she kept quiet.

The arrived to the headstone, a standard issue dome like all the others. It should have been a private moment, but it wasn't. Even though they appeared to be alone, several soldiers had been posted discreetly in a tight perimeter around them.

Tyler broke the silence and read the caption. *"Collin St. Germain. Corporal. USMC. Gulf War. August 3, 1972 to May 14, 2008. Highest Honor of Sacrifice."* He took the maroon rose from the notch in his jacket and bent down to tuck the stem into the sand surrounding it. "Rest in peace, Collin." The tremor in his voice echoed the tears running down his cheek.

The ground under Lauren swirled as she rocked forward. Her head dropped into her hands and Tyler barely caught her by the elbows as she crumpled to her knees. At least he was there to break that fall. He took a step back so she could melt and covered her with his jacket, shielding her from them as much as possible.

Broken.

When her crying mellowed to a few sporadic hiccups, Tyler knelt on one knee and gingerly placed his hand on her back. "Let's sit down at that gazebo and catch our breath."

Her shirt was wet when he helped her up, but his dark jacket hid whatever fluid might be seeping onto her silky top.

Under the wooden dome, she perched on the edge of the bench and pulled a fresh bandage from her purse. She slid it under her top and pressed it on her side.

"It hurts, doesn't it?" Tyler inquired softly.

"Yes. But I am sweating like crazy, seriously soaked all the way though."

"Oh, my God, I thought you were bleeding. I thought I needed to rush you to the hospital or something after this."

She dropped her head with a smile. "Jesus, D, how did we get here?"

"How bad is all this?" He motioned to her, his hand moving up and down her physique.

She reached for one more bandage and secured it under her top to soak sweat from her other armpit as well. She laid his jacket on the bench and shifted to a more comfortable position. "Shrapnel is some viscous stuff...rusty, sharp, metal fragments, like bolts, nails, screws, ball bearings...all kinds of shit. Whatever they can get their hands on. It's all burning hot from the explosion, but that's irrelevant when the stuff rips through your flesh at the speed of a bullet. Totally rung my bell. And the ambulance people—fuckers—they cuffed me down. At least they got the needle in on the first stab.

Oh, and on the drive to Beaumont, they…the EMTs, that's the word…. They had to speak loudly, like almost yell, because of the sirens. The last thing I thought was, *Why don't they use headsets?* And then…nothing. For like, two days."

Lauren glanced at Tyler's jacket. "Do you still smoke?"

"No."

"So, there were three surgeries to scrape most of the metal out and they grafted skin from my thigh to replace what had been ripped off here." She motioned to her left rib. "They kept me on the floor reserved for prisoners at Beaumont—that's the VA hospital here—'til I could be taken to DC and stand trial. There was an armed guard posted to my door twenty-four seven at the hospital, not to keep people out…." She cocked an eyebrow. "Anyway, after three go rounds of surgery and skin grafting, the doctors determined any remaining pieces of shrapnel still lodged into the flesh around my hips could just stay there since it wasn't hurting the bones."

She came up for air.

"Four of my ribs were broken and everything healed up, but other things started to change inside of me. I didn't know how else to explain it, I just kept telling the doctor that those shards of metal they left inside my hips felt radioactive. Sounds crazy, right? But it was the only word I could come up with, so they did a bunch of Xrays and determined it was psychosomatic. They had the shrink assigned to me—a Major named Miller—break it down like this: 'As you move through your grief, Lauren, you'll find that uncomfortable sensation will also decrease.' I'd still like to fucking deck her."

Tyler gazed across the sea of headstones. "Maybe we can find you a shrink in L.A."

"I need to tell you something."

His eyes flicked to hers and then back away. Whatever came next was going to be heavy enough, there was no need to intensify the moment by boring down on her with eye contact.

"Sometimes I feel like the shrapnel—the metal left in my hips from the blast—I think it's communicating with something outside of me. Like a transceiver that picks up signals from demons that whisper into my thoughts. They…." She paused, trying to find the right word, "They worry me, and when I can't bear it anymore, they promise to take it all away—the pain, the memories, Collin's death…everything. All I need to do is 'make a wish….'"

Tyler didn't react. It had been years since they've had contact, and one of the first questions he asked her was if Collin had brainwashed her or if this was shellshock.

"I know it sounds crazy and I don't expect you to believe me, but if something happens to me, it's because of that. I'm cursed."

"Do you think something bad is going to happen to you?"

"Something bad is happening to me."

"You're right. I'm sorry, I don't know what to say."

"When Collin died, the demon—Iblis—the red one that haunted him when he was a kid, IT left him and came right over to me. It kicked me between the legs, right where I kicked Collin in marriage counseling...."

"What?" Tyler looked to her in disbelief.

"It was nothing...it was both of us. Don't you understand what I'm saying? I inherited Collin's curse."

Tyler tapped his fingers on the bench as if drumming up a way to get this girl's head straight. "The shrapnel, the surgeries, how is the recovery going? Are you able to move around much? Have you thought about easing yourself back into a gentle yoga practice?"

Tyler's obvious pivot let her down.

"I already have."

He nodded and checked his watch. "It's time, Lauren."

"I don't want to say goodbye to him now. And the ironic thing? That's all I wanted to do before he died."

It must have been the pleading tone coming through her voice that caused Tyler to ask if her meds were wearing off.

"What if they're right? What if I really did miss something on Yilmaz? I could have prevented all this."

Tyler reached around to snatch up her purse and fished around for her pain meds. "You did not make those bombs live. You are not responsible for Collin's death. You cannot keep going down this road." Tyler sucked in a gasp when he read the label on her pills. It was a prescription for a Fentanyl and Ketamine mix. With refills. He set a long, hard look on her before offering some comfort. "He knows you love him. Nothing is perfect all the time between anyone, but that doesn't take away from the real love between you two." He handed her one. "Can you dry swallow?"

The sun had dipped down in the sky and it was the time of day when the white moon made its appearance on the other side of the sky.

"Let's make our way back to that conflicted soldier," she said and stood.

The wrought iron gates peeled apart for the government issued vehicle to edge through the swarm pushing against it. It was on its way to the small airfield in Santa Theresa, New Mexico, to drop off its passengers at a private plane chartered by PuraYoga. But before the car had even cleared the crowd, Lauren dropped her head on Tyler's shoulder, exhausted from the day.

He bluntly elbowed her in the side. "Buck up. And sit up straight. You won't make it to the other side of this any other way."

An hour later, with a bottle of water and a strong cocktail of meds digesting, Lauren lazily messed around on her phone while the Flight Captain performed his pre-checks. "Tyler," she said as she held her screen in front of him, "this is what I was talking about. It says here that if revenge sought on a living target by the djinn and that target dies, then the curse is inherited by the next of kin."

Tyler looked up from his own phone with a bemused expression. "You need to stop it with this talk of curses and genies. Have you been through hell and back? Yes. Is there a supernatural puppet master? No. People, including Collin, will reach for anything just to make it seem like there's meaning behind all this. Give me your phone and take a whole Xanax for the flight. We're going to wean you off that horse tranquilizer shit. The Xanax will help. The last of the furniture's been delivered and Thom had the guys get rid of all the boxes. He even washed the sheets and made up your bed. I'll pick up a new phone for you once we land."

e p i l o g u e

James counted backwards on his fingertips. "That was three months before I met you."

I nodded with a smile at the thought of that first time we met on the ship. Here we were, the Monday after Thanksgiving watching the sun go down and now...well, now he knew everything.

His phone vibrated. It took less than ten seconds for him to check it, fling it back on the corner of the blanket, and abruptly get up to shove off down the beach without saying a word.

Matt: *2 episodes in the first season with an option for a recurring role in the second. Best we can do.*
11/30/2009, 5:01 p.m.

I sighed.
There's no getting out of Africa now.

military terminology

The military has its own language of insider phrases and slang terms. The use of acronyms in professional dialogue is expected, as is the ability to understand. This is a list of terms used in *The Path of Least Resistance* that might be unfamiliar to readers outside the spheres in which Collin and Lauren work.

o 1 A/D: First Armored Division nicknamed "Old Ironsides"
o 3-1: Third Brigade Combat Team, Infantry Division
o A, B, C, or D level issues: Classification of issues raised in a background investigation ranging from minor to major.
o AAR: After Action Report
o AAV: Amphibious Assault Vehicle
o ACD: Assigned Completion Date, deadline for an investigator to complete field work and turn in an official report to an adjudicator.
o AD: Armored Division
o ADA: Air Defense Artillery
o BP: Border Patrol

- Booz Allen Hamilton: "Booz" One of the largest government contractors.
- C4: A common variety of plastic explosives.
- CAC card: Common Access Card, ID required to be on a person at all times while on a military base.
- CBP: Customs and Border Protection Agency
- CD: Date that an adjudicator needs to make a ruling on a case.
- CONUS: Contiguous United States
- "creds": Short for credentials.
- DD214: Discharge form that details a veteran's record of service.
- DHS: Department of Homeland Security
- DLI: Defense Language Institute
- DOA: Department of the Army
- DOD: Department of Defense
- E-4: The fourth enlisted rank in the US military.
- EMT: Emergency Medical Technician
- EOD: Explosive Ordinance Disposal
- EPPD: El Paso Police Department
- ESI: Extended Subject Interview
- East Bliss: The most recent expansion of Fort Bliss.
- FOB: Forward Operating Base
- FPCON Level Delta: Force Protection Condition describing the state of a military site when a terrorist attack is taking place; complete lockdown.

- GS plates: License plates assigned to government-owned vehicles.
- "going down range": Slang meaning to literally move down the training range, or lane, toward a target.
- "going to theater": Deploying to a large area of operations.
- HME Lab: Homemade Explosives Lab
- Holmes creds: Code name for a classified contract and the associated credentials needed to work on it.
- IA: Internal Affairs
- ICE: Immigrations and Customs Enforcement
- IED: Improvised Explosive Device, an unconventional bomb made from available materials and used by unofficial forces a.k.a. roadside bomb.
- IEDES: Improvised Explosive Device Effect Simulator
- JPAS: Joint Personnel Adjudication System
- J Plane: Janet Plane, a recognizable aircraft that transports employees back and forth from McCarren airport in Las Vegas to Groom Lake/Area 51 on a daily basis.
- Kamal Jabour: A mock Middle Eastern village built at Fort Bliss that is used for training purposes.
- MCLC: Mine Clearing Line Charge
- MOS: Military Occupational Specialty
- MP: Military Police

- McGregor Range: Pre-deployment training area and live-fire weapons range outside of Fort Bliss.
- Mod 99: Modification notification that a change has been made in the OPM handbook.
- NCO: Non-Commissioned Officer
- NLT: No later than
- NSA: National Security Agency
- OPM: Office of Personnel Management
- OT: Overtime
- PIPS: Personnel Investigating Processing System
- POW: Prisoner of War
- PTSD: Post-Traumatic Stress Disorder
- Patriot Missile: US anti-missile defense system made famous during Operation Desert Storm.
- Privacy Act of 1974: States that all information collected on an individual shall be made available to that individual upon written request.
- *Project Red One*: Code name for a classified project that utilizes spiritual warfare to obtain unique intelligence.
- Protected Source: A source whose identity has been kept secret.
- ROTC: Reserve Officers' Training Corps
- "re-up"- Slang for the periodic re-investigations conducted every five years on an individual once they obtain a clearance.

- SF: Special Forces, military units used to perform unconventional missions.
- SF-86: Standard Form 86, an extensive intake questionnaire filled out by a person seeking a security clearance.
- SIM Card: Subscriber Identification Module, used to identify and authenticate subscribers on mobile devices
- SME: Subject Matter Expert
- SO: Security Officer
- Sight Verify: When an investigator is required to inspect a document in person.
- Source: Person being interviewed as a reference for a subject.
- Subject: Person under investigation.
- TC: Track Commander
- TDY: Temporary Duty Assignment
- TS: Top Secret Clearance
- TSA: Transportation Security Administration
- Talon: Tracked Military Robot
- Task Force Ripper: One of multiple Marine Corps groups assembled during Operation Desert Storm to liberate Kuwait from the occupying Iraqi forces.
- The Lab: Slang for Los Alamos.
- Tobin Wells: ADA and IED training area in the raw desert just outside of Fort Bliss proper.
- VA: Veterans Affairs

- VFW: Veterans of Foreign Wars
- VSB: Virtual Battle Space
- WBAMC "Beaumont": William Beaumont Army Medical Center
- WMD FBI: Weapons of Mass Destruction, Federal Bureau of Investigations
- WSMR "Wizzmer": White Sands Missile Range

The Path of Most Resistance

Preview of Book III

OPERATION LIGHTINING THUNDER: The Ugandan government had just officially stated that the Lord's Resistance Army's (LRA) main camp, deep in Garamba National Forest, has been burned to the ground.

December 21, 2008

The waning crescent moon made no allowances for any extra light to see by as Joseph Kony's second in command, Philippe Ongwen, strained to make out the face of his pocket compass. Using a flashlight was not an option, even though it had been several hours since he'd assured Kony, the leader of the LRA, that no one—absolutely no one—was capable of tracking him. Philippe didn't want to risk being seen should there be another loner lurking in the jungle.

Philippe's mission was to locate a nondescript spot deep in the Garamba forest, where a cache of weapons had been buried by the LRA a year prior. He was to then take the bundle to Kony's hideout. Philippe hadn't anticipated it would take him so long to reach the secluded location, a mere two miles from the now destroyed LRA base camp. It was dark and he began to second guess his calculations. The jungle was overgrown and seemed thicker than he recalled.

He crouched down to catch his breath and reevaluate his surroundings.

His brain raced through the last exchange he'd had with Kony, just moments prior to camouflaging himself to blend into the forest. Philippe fled from the confusion with relief to be out in the jungle on his own.

Unfortunately, there hadn't been enough time to formulate a proper escape plan for the rest of them. By the time Kony was tipped off about the advancing troops, the frontline of Sudanese, Congolese, and Ugandan forces was less than an hour away. Philippe heard that the US president, George W. Bush, had signed a treaty to provide financial support to the African joint task.

The last order given to Philippe was in the form of a shout from Kony, "Get the bag, our backup!" followed by a knowing look. One that told him to go straight to the hideout after obtaining the hidden arms.

The last thought gave him a start of urgency and he jumped to his feet. On the hunt again, he confidently strode forward, not caring if he was on the right path. He just wanted to be in motion.

Within a split second, the ground fell out from below his feet and his senses were eclipsed by sheer pain. Unable to stifle his reaction, he howled.

Philippe had stepped into a pitfall trap, one that his own troops had built to capture elephants, and fell on top of a sizeable spear. The spear tips had all been coated with poison and the one that skewered his left thigh immobilized him. The burning sensation that spread through his body was unlike any pain he'd ever experienced.

Two red eyes peered down on him.

"Help me!" Philippe screamed at the figure looming over the hole.

IT didn't respond, but floated down to look Philippe dead in the eyes.

Philippe was going into shock.

"We can make a deal. The pain can end immediately, but in return…." IT trailed off.

Panting, Philippe gasped at what could have easily been his final words. "Anything! I'll do anything!"

"An introduction to your leader will suffice. A young woman and her star are coming to your forest to thwart the efforts of the LRA. Kony will want to know about the couple."

The Path of Least Resistance

Reading Group Guide

For more information about *Catch a Falling Star* and *The Path of Least Resistance*, please visit Leah Downing's Author Page on Facebook.

☐ What inspired Collin to speak out during LtCol Mattis's briefing the night prior to the US Liberation of Kuwait? What could have been the reason behind LtCol Mattis's decision to switch the direction of assault based solely on one young Marine's concern regarding the original path?

☐ How does government contractor involvement in US wars and conflicts make the US military's mission more complex?

☐ When Collin first meets Lauren, he is sensitive to her hesitation about drinking from an already open bottle at a club, yet at the Hard Rock pool, he witnesses a couple of guys dosing beers with GHB (or some other date-rape drug), and grants them the go-ahead to give one to her. What factors are at play?

☐ As details regarding the St. Germain curse are revealed, what can be surmised about the development of Collin's mistrust of women? If indeed no supernatural force were behind it, but he was told as a child that he was destined to marry a beautiful, but adulterous woman, would a supernatural influence even be relevant?

- Could Iblis have merely been a figment of Collin's imagination?
- Is it possible that Collin latched onto the idea of this curse as a crutch, a get-out-of-free card for controlling behavior?
- Does Stephanie know about Iblis and the curse?

☐ In both *Catch a Falling Star* and *The Path of Least Resistance*, individuals used drugs to connect with Iblis, both intentionally and unintentionally. How does this affect the reliability of a story as told from a character who was in an altered state?

☐ During his last few moments of life, Mayhem confesses that angels initiated the fuse on the ignitor, allowing the second line charge to explode when his attempt failed. What are some other sections in *The Path of Least Resistance* that touch upon angel symbolism?

☐ Do you think that Charles is Collin's son? Why or why not?

☐ Many cultures believe that unusual behaviors, those that are often symptomatic of mental health issues, are caused by spirit possession. Collin's relationship with Iblis could be written off as a psychotic disorder. What would his diagnosis be if it was believed that he was mentally ill and not cursed?

☐ Is Tyler a true friend to Lauren?

THE PATH OF LEAST RESISTANCE